"If you do something for me, in return I will buy the *castillo*, settle all its debts and turn it into a profit-making enterprise. I will even offer you a stake, if you'd like."

Eva couldn't quite compute this information for a long moment. She'd been facing the prospect of sizable debts remaining even after the sale. But these would be gone. *And* he was offering her a business opportunity?

Then she recalled what he'd said and immediately she was suspicious. "What do you want me to do for you?"

Vidal folded his arms. "I want you to agree to a public engagement with me."

Vidal watched Eva closely. Seeing her like this in a maid's uniform had thrown him. More than thrown him. He'd underestimated how impoverished she was. And yet, not for a moment had she let that hauteur slip.

Eva looked a little stunned. And then confused. "A public engagement...like an event?"

"No. Like a marriage engagement."

Eva went white. Something about her reaction made Vidal feel simultaneously insulted and vindicated by the impulsive decision he'd made.

"You want to marry me?" she asked, sounding shocked.

Irish author **Abby Green** ended a very glamorous career in film and TV—which really consisted of a lot of standing in the rain outside actors' trailers—to pursue her love of romance. After she'd bombarded Harlequin with manuscripts, they kindly accepted one, and an author was born. She lives in Dublin, Ireland, and loves any excuse for distraction. Visit abby-green.com or email abbygreenauthor@gmail.com.

Books by Abby Green

Harlequin Presents

The Greek's Unknown Bride
Bound by Her Shocking Secret

Passionately Ever After...

The Kiss She Claimed from the Greek

Hot Summer Nights with a Billionaire

The Flaw in His Red-Hot Revenge

The Marchetti Dynasty

The Maid's Best Kept Secret
The Innocent Behind the Scandal
Bride Behind the Desert Veil

Jet-Set Billionaires

Their One-Night Rio Reunion

Visit the Author Profile page
at Harlequin.com for more titles.

Abby Green

A RING FOR THE
SPANIARD'S REVENGE

ISBN-13: 978-1-335-58401-4

A Ring for the Spaniard's Revenge

Copyright © 2022 by Abby Green

Recycling programs for this product may not exist in your area.

This is a work of fiction. Names, characters, places and incidents are either the product of the author's imagination or are used fictitiously. Any resemblance to actual persons, living or dead, businesses, companies, events or locales is entirely coincidental.

For questions and comments about the quality of this book, please contact us at CustomerService@Harlequin.com.

Harlequin Enterprises ULC
22 Adelaide St. West, 41st Floor
Toronto, Ontario M5H 4E3, Canada
www.Harlequin.com

Printed in U.S.A.

A RING FOR THE SPANIARD'S REVENGE

This is for my beautiful niece,
Brída Mernagh Spee. A ray of light and love who
arrived into our lives when we needed it most.

CHAPTER ONE

Castillo de Santos, outside Madrid

Eva Flores shivered, even though the sun was shining and the early autumn temperature was balmy. She should be feeling relieved. Happy, even. But she wasn't even sure she knew what *happy* felt like, because it had never been a dominant emotion for her. She knew she'd only ever felt it on distinct occasions.

Before she could ruminate on that unpalatable revelation, she figured that she could work with relieved. Beyond relieved. After a year of trying to sell the *castillo* she'd grown up in, the only home she'd ever known, a potential buyer had finally materialised.

He was due to come and visit now, as a precursor to signing the contracts, and when she'd expressed concern the solicitor had assured her, 'He is very interested. He's the kind of man who wouldn't be taking time out of his busy schedule if he hadn't already made up his mind. He just wants to do this as a formality.'

Still, Eva couldn't help trying to temper her relief with a bit of caution. He hadn't signed yet, and until he did this crumbling mausoleum was still hers, with all its bleak memories, loneliness and massive debts.

The *castillo* had felt like a prison for a long time and it effectively still was. Binding her here until she could get rid of it.

She was walking through the rambling gardens, long since neglected and overgrown since the last member of staff had left.

Eva's gut clenched. She definitely didn't want to go down *that* memory lane. Much better to focus on the fact that soon she could begin her life in earnest and try to put her past behind her.

This place had claimed too much of her time. And yet she still felt a compulsion to walk its paths, as if to lay some ghost to rest. *The ghost of her mother.* A familiar swell of something far more complicated than just plain grief rose up inside Eva. It was grief and anger and a sense of futility. Her mother had dictated Eva's life in such a controlling way that it was only through her death that Eva had been able to get some perspective and enough space to start figuring out who she was.

She halted now at the rusted wrought-iron gate

that led into a small walled garden with a fountain in the centre. Eva stepped inside and the heady scent of blooms in their last throes filled her nostrils.

Weeds ran rampant through the cracks in the stones on the ground and in every nook and cranny of the brick walls. She should feel guilty that it had gone to such waste but all she felt was empty. Numb.

She turned around slowly to see the elaborately decorated gazebo in a corner, almost hidden by foliage. A beautiful and whimsical piece of architecture that some previous ancestor had had installed. It certainly hadn't been her parents, who had shared no love at all. Her father had eventually walked out and left them when Eva was eight.

That act had thrown her mother into a deep pit of bitterness and despair and had made her toxic. She'd turned to Eva and used her as an object to project all her betrayal and towering rage, seeing in her daughter an opportunity to make sure she was never hurt in the same way. And so far, Eva could attest, she hadn't been. So maybe her mother's legacy had worked.

After all, it wasn't as if she'd had an opportunity to meet anyone in order to *be* hurt.

Except for—

She shut down her mind. Thinking of him

caused a maelstrom of emotions that Eva didn't want to investigate. It always had, ever since she'd first laid eyes on him when she was a teenager. Tall and more beautiful than anything she'd ever seen in her life. Even then she'd known that he connected with her in a way that scared her and that she didn't fully understand.

Her mother had seen it, though. She'd found Eva watching him out of the window one day when he'd been working in the garden. Shirtless. Olive skin gleaming. Strong muscles flexing.

Her mother had drawn her close and said, 'A boy like him is driven purely by brute desires, Eva. You are worth so much more than him. But that doesn't mean you can't remind him of that...'

She'd had no idea what her mother was talking about, but it had become apparent over the years. Her mother had wanted her to entice him. To provoke those brute desires so she could rise above them and laugh at him. To remind him of his place and the fact that she was totally unattainable.

The only problem was that he hadn't been a brute. Far from it. He'd been studious, polite and...*sexy.* Eva had become progressively more and more aware of him, so that by that last summer, when she'd turned eighteen, she'd felt like a tinder box about to blow up with surging desires and aching needs and emotions far too confusing for her to know how to handle.

So she hadn't handled them.

The last time she'd seen him had been here in this space...when it had looked as it should.

She could still remember him, so tall and powerful. Short dark hair. Serious expression. Looking at her with a mixture of wariness, pity and anger. It had enflamed her. She'd desperately wanted to provoke a reaction. And she had.

Her skin prickled at the memory. Unconsciously she curled her fingers over her palms. She could still feel the heat of anger and rage and, worse, the shock of what she'd almost done. The way he'd looked at her with disgust. She'd never felt so raw. So...lost.

She cursed herself for letting her imagination run amok into the past. Today was about the future. And she realised she was mooning around the grounds still dressed in worn jeans, an even more worn shirt and scuffed sneakers. With her hair pulled back messily, she didn't look remotely like the owner of a crumbling *castillo*. If she could still be called an owner when the bank really owned it all.

It was a sorry state of affairs for the last person in the line descending from her mother's illustrious family.

She knew she was the last, because she never

intended to have children. Not after what she'd experienced. The thought of having a child sent a sense of terror through her at the thought that she might subject them to what she'd been subjected to. Even with the best will in the world.

Enough. She had to get ready.

She turned around to leave the garden but came to an abrupt halt when she saw someone standing in the gateway. Someone very tall and broad. Masculine. The sun was in her eyes, though, and she couldn't make out his features.

This had to be the potential buyer…but how had he found this garden? The grounds were labyrinthine even to her, and she'd lived here her whole life.

For some reason she felt a shiver of recognition. She put a hand up to try and block the sun. 'Hello. Can I help you?'

The man stepped forward and she realised he was even taller than she'd first thought. Well over six foot. And then she saw his face and the blood stopped coursing through her veins.

It couldn't be.

The man took off his sunglasses, revealing all too familiar deep-set eyes an unusual colour of green and blue. Aquamarine. They'd always reminded Eva of the sea.

When he spoke his voice was deep. 'Hello, Eva. We meet again.'

Eva reeled. Had she conjured him up out of her imagination? Literally willed him into existence?

He wore a suit that was moulded to his very powerful body. She'd never seen him in a suit. It had always been jeans or shorts and T-shirts. Now she was the one in jeans and a shirt—the kind of clothes she had been forbidden from ever wearing. She'd rarely been out of them in the past year, in a sort of very belated and ineffectual rebellion.

'Vidal Suarez…' She breathed the name she hadn't even wanted to think of a few moments ago. She didn't realise she'd spoken out loud.

'You do remember me, then.'

Always. The word popped into Eva's head and she clamped her mouth shut in case it fell out. Except the person she remembered had been a young man on the cusp of his power. Lean and muscular. Not this…this fully formed man.

'I… What are you doing here?'

He stepped closer and looked around. She could hardly comprehend that it was him. She felt confused, wondered if the sun was getting to her.

He said musingly, as if it was entirely normal for him to be there, 'I always liked this space. Shame it's gone to seed.' He looked at her. 'But then you and your mother always did have a careless attitude to the *castillo* and its upkeep.'

She wasn't imagining him. His words sliced into her. It had been her mother who had relished the ruination of the *castillo*. As if the disintegrating state of their home might make her father realise that he had made a huge mistake and come back to make amends, fearful of what people would say. But he hadn't. And the *castillo* had continued to slowly decline. In spite of the skeleton staff's efforts to keep it somewhat respectable.

His words seemed to break her out of her trance. 'What are you doing here?' she repeated.

'Aren't you expecting me?'

Too many things impacted upon Eva at once for her to be able to assimilate them all. The implication of what he was saying was too huge to take in.

'I'm waiting for someone from Sol Enterprises.'

'Sol Enterprises is my company.'

Eva shook her head. 'But…how…? Why?'

But even as she asked the question a memory came back. This same man, seven years ago, saying, *'Some are born to this kind of privilege, Eva, and some have to earn it, but I think it's safe to say that the earning of it is so much more sat-*

isfying. For all your privilege, you don't strike me as particularly grateful or happy.'

The clarity of the memory mocked her.

Vidal was looking at her carefully, and the shock of his appearance made her feel as if the walls of the garden were closing in around her. For one awful moment Eva felt light-headed and thought she might faint. But it passed. She had to move away from here.

She skirted around Vidal Suarez and said, 'We should go to the house.'

'Yes, that would be good.'

As Eva walked down the well-worn paths ahead of him she forced herself to take deep breaths. She'd never expected to see Vidal Suarez again. His life now was so far removed from where she was and from where he'd been.

By the time he had come to the *castillo* with his grounds manager father at the age of twenty he had already been known locally as a prodigiously talented boy who had won a prestigious scholarship to one of Spain's most exclusive schools, and had then gone on to win yet more scholarships to the world's best universities.

It was probably the reason Eva's mother had allowed him to live here with his father—as long as he helped out during his holidays, of course. For free.

And now he was a billionaire—a tech entrepreneur who had blazed a trail across the world before settling in San Francisco, the global hub of tech innovation.

Eva's mother had taken great pleasure in making Vidal do menial work alongside his father, as if to remind him of his true place. But that last summer Eva had seen him had been the summer his life had changed. He'd made his first million.

Years after the Suarezes had left the *castillo*, and as their own fortune had declined, her mother—who had been following Vidal's well-documented stratospheric progress—had said to Eva, 'You should go to him…ask him for help. He owes us.'

Eva had turned on her mother and said, with barely controlled fury, 'He owes us nothing, Mother. Nothing.'

We owe him. I owe him. She hadn't said it, but she'd thought it.

She could almost feel the weight of Vidal Suarez judging the sorry state of the gardens behind her. She felt guilty, even though there was nothing she could have done about it. All her energy had been taken up in keeping herself and the *castillo* afloat. Not that it had done much good in the end.

Her mother had refused to sell. Had refused to show any sign that she'd struggled since her husband had left her all those years before. Preferring to live in a state of total inertia and denial.

It was only after she'd died that Eva had been able to take control, but that sense of control was suddenly very elusive as questions abounded in her head: *Why him? Why now?*

She had no idea why Vidal Suarez had come back here now, potentially to buy the *castillo*. Or maybe she did and she just didn't want to acknowledge the gut-churning evidence that he hadn't forgotten or forgiven his treatment at her hands. At her mother's hands.

They approached the *castillo* from the front, where a large circular area featured another elaborate fountain that lay sadly dry and empty. A sleek, low-slung sports car—presumably Vidal's—looked incongruous against the shabby backdrop.

The *castillo* itself was an imposing building, a mix of classical and Moorish design. The dramatic arching entrance led into an open courtyard, with pillars around the edges.

Another memory blasted back at that moment—as if Eva needed reminding. Her mother had invited Vidal to join them for dinner one evening. Eva had been mortifyingly excited. Sixteen and full of hormones, and giddy with a desire she'd had no idea how to handle.

Vidal had arrived and he'd clearly made an

effort. Eva had thought he'd never looked more handsome in chinos and a shirt. Hair smoothed back. Smelling of musk and earthy spices.

And then her mother had proceeded to talk to Eva about Vidal for the entire evening as if he wasn't there. As if he was a specimen to discuss and not a human being to have a conversation with. As if he was sub-human.

It had been excruciating, and Eva had burned with shame and anger. But even then she hadn't been brave enough to stand up to her mother. She'd pulled invisible armour around herself, so nothing could touch her and she could hide. Hide her feelings and desires.

Vidal had suffered that insulting dinner with innate pride and a politeness they hadn't deserved. He hadn't joined them again.

And now he was here, supposedly interested in buying the *castillo*. It shouldn't be surprising at all that he was taking an opportunity to dish out a little humiliation of his own. The only surprise was that he hadn't put all this behind him. That he wanted anything to do with the *castillo* and Eva, at all.

Eva led him into the main reception room and winced inwardly at the even sorrier state of affairs inside the *castillo*. Peeling wallpaper, damp patches, threadbare oriental rugs… Portraits of ancestors covered in dirt. Dust sheets strewn over a lot of the furniture—not that they were helping much.

Eva steeled herself to face him again before she turned around, but it didn't work very well. Any steel seemed to turn to liquid as she drank him in—this time without the sun in her eyes.

With his powerful build, short dark hair— almost militarily short—and hard-boned face dominated by those wide deep-set eyes, he oozed a raw vitality that effortlessly eclipsed the crumbling *castillo* behind him.

The clipped dark beard that hugged his jaw only drew attention to his mouth. A wide mouth, with lips generous enough to look almost pretty.

But they hadn't felt pretty. They'd felt hard.

Eva's heart thumped.

Please, not those memories. Not now.

'You're looking at me as if you've never seen me before,' he said.

Eva felt heat rise. 'You look…different.'

'I am different.'

There was a stern tone to his voice that made Eva realise just how much had changed for him. Coming from a humble background, he'd well and truly surpassed all expectations. His wealth was inestimable and apparently he owned real estate in every major city. There was even a bolt-hole in Hawaii.

Eva wondered if he thought *she* had changed.

She felt changed. Bruised and weary after a lifetime of being told what to think and how to behave. She felt vulnerable. As if a protective layer
of skin was gone.

That made her conscious of her clothes, and
she gestured to herself. 'I was going to change
before…' she hesitated '…before you came.'

Those green-blue eyes drifted down and up
again. A pulse throbbed deep in Eva's body. A
pulse of awareness and something being brought
back to life. *Her.* In his presence. As if she'd
been dormant until now.

'Not your usual attire…? But then how would
I know? It's been a long time. Evidently the de-
mise of the *castillo* hasn't been confined to the
building.'

'I think it's pretty obvious that things aren't…
the same.'

Vidal took his gaze off her and Eva felt as if
she could breathe again. He looked around the
space, his hands in the pockets of his trousers.
Then he looked back at her. 'Things are different. I can't lie and pretend I liked your mother
all that much, but I am sorry for your loss.'

Those tangled emotions churned in Eva's gut.
She hid them and lifted her chin, saying in a
clipped voice, 'Thank you.'

Vidal shook his head. 'You're still a cold one,
I see. Not even a mention of your mother gets

you to display a chink of emotion. You two were as thick as thieves.'

Eva looked at him and was genuinely lost for words. How could he think that? *Because it was true,* whispered a voice. Yes, it had been true in one sense. She'd been a captive audience and acolyte for her mother. 'Captive' being the operative word.

She forced a brittle smile. 'It's a funny thing, perspective, isn't it?' In a bid to get him away from the subject of her mother, she asked, 'How is your father?'

Vidal's hands came out of his pockets. His expression hardened. 'You're saying you don't know?'

Eva frowned. 'Know what?' All she knew were these neglected walls and gardens and the route she took to her job every day in Madrid.

'That he's dead.' Vidal's voice was flat.

Eva balked and struggled to speak for a moment, eventually getting out, 'But…how? When?'

'As if you care.'

She felt defensive. 'I always liked your father. He was kind.'

'More kind than you and your mother deserved.'

Shame coiled in Eva's belly. She recalled a moment when she'd delivered an instruction to Vidal's father on behalf of her mother, who had told her never to talk to him as if he were their equal. After delivering the message, she'd walked away—only to be stopped in her tracks by Vidal.

The sheer surprise of seeing him had had a flush of awareness rising through her body before she'd been able to stop it. The kind of thing her mother had warned her about. Being at the mercy of her emotions...hormones. All weaknesses.

Vidal had looked angry. 'Who do you think you are to talk to your senior like that?'

A mix of hot emotions at his reprimand had made Eva's chest feel tight. Shame and confusion and something much more complicated. Something she hadn't understood, even at sixteen years of age. And so she'd retreated behind that cool indifference her mother had taught her so well and lifted her chin the way she'd watched her mother do it. 'Who do you think *you* are to talk to *me* like this? You're not even an employee here. The fact that you're here at all is because of the generosity of my mother.'

Even as the words had fallen out of her mouth they'd felt acrid. Wrong. But it had been safer to hide behind them than allow Vidal to see the awful churning mix of emotions inside her. The shame.

Vidal had shaken his head. 'You're a piece of work—do you know that? Here in your castle that's falling to the ground, clinging onto nothing but a name and empty privilege. You're pathetic. Don't talk to my father like that again.'

For a horrifying moment Eva had felt hot tears threaten, and she'd known immediately that she was weak. So she'd forced all the emotion down and locked it in ice and said, 'You do not have the right to tell me what to do.' And she'd walked away before Vidal could say another word and bring all those emotions to the surface again.

Eva swallowed the shameful and painful memory. 'How…? When did he die?'

'Not long after he left the *castillo.*'

'But that was about five years ago. Was he ill?'

Vidal's voice was stark. 'He was proud. Too proud to leave his job even though I could support him. He felt some misguided loyalty to you and your mother. Even though she felt nothing similar and let him go with no notice and no compensation. I was in the United States. I offered for him to come and join me, but he didn't want to be "a burden". His words. The cancer was already very advanced and in his pancreas by the time the doctors diagnosed it. He died within months. There was nothing I could do.'

'I'm so sorry. I had no idea.' Eva felt nauseous.

'Why would you? He'd only ever been a faceless, nameless employee to you and your mother. He'd had symptoms of his illness while working at the *castillo* but your mother refused to let him have time off to get checked out. And he didn't want to make a fuss.'

Eva remembered the day Vidal's father had left. He had looked suddenly much older. Clearly in shock at the abrupt nature of his departure. She'd offered to help him, but he had insisted that he was fine and her mother had told her to let him go.

Too many memories. This was what Eva was hoping to get away from by selling the *castillo*. Being forced to relive the past.

She folded her arms across her chest. 'Vidal, why are you really here?'

Why are you really here? Why was he here, indeed? An answer floated into his head before he could stop it. *Because you couldn't forget about her.*

Nonsense, he assured himself. He actually did have a plan for this *castillo*, and it had nothing to do with Eva Flores.

Are you sure about that? mocked his conscience.

He couldn't ignore the distinct sizzle in his blood. And it wasn't so much a sizzle as a lick of flame along every vein. Flames that made his skin tighten with awareness and need.

For this woman? After all this time? Galling. Irritating. He hadn't thought about her in years.

Liar.

Vidal grimaced inwardly. If he was being totally honest, she had slid back into his consciousness from time to time. Usually at inopportune moments when he was with a woman and he suddenly found himself thinking of Eva's cool beauty and haughty airs, wondering where she was and if she was still an ice queen, incapable of cracking even a smile to indicate any kind of warmth.

He could imagine men being fascinated enough to want to see if they could be the one to melt all that ice and find the woman underneath. Because, for a time, he'd fantasised about that. Much as he'd like to deny it.

And now that he was standing in front of her she was both exactly what he'd expected and *not.* But he couldn't put his finger on the difference. She was as beautiful as ever. More so, having grown into her coltish limbs and womanly curves.

Maybe it was the fact that she was dressed down. He'd never seen her less than immaculately put together, even though he'd rarely seen her leave the *castillo* with her mother.

She had been home-schooled. He'd used to feel sorry for her, thinking of her as some kind of hothouse flower kept apart from society, but inevitably if he'd said anything remotely resembling pity or compassion she'd come back with a withering put-down and made Vidal feel like a fool for assuming she was like other mortals.

She wasn't. She was a product of her illustrious lineage and she'd been born to make strategic connections and alliances. As she'd liked to remind him.

His father had used to say to him, 'Just ignore her, son. She doesn't even know what she's doing.'

But Vidal had always suspected otherwise. And he'd been right if that last encounter had been anything to go by, on her eighteenth birthday. She might not have been worldly but she'd known of her effect on him, and she'd done everything in her power to ensure he noticed her so that she could then punish him for it.

She'd moved through the grounds of that *castillo* with all the regal aloofness of a queen inspecting her troops and finding them lacking. She'd found Vidal lacking. Especially when he had refused her.

He could still feel her slim body against his, trembling with desperation. Skinny arms winding around his neck, and that pouting spoiled mouth pressed to his.

At the shocking sensation of all that soft sweetness, so at odds with her very *un*-soft personality, Vidal had almost lost it. He'd almost forgotten who she was and how she'd tormented him. That she was nowhere near worldly enough to take what was bubbling up inside him. A heat so intense that it had almost fused his brain cells. *Almost.*

He'd pulled back and taken her arms in his hands. Pushed her away. She'd looked at him with wide, shocked eyes. Molten brown. Golden. Colour slashed along those aristocratic cheekbones. Silky dark hair had been falling loose from her ponytail.

And there was something else he hadn't seen before. A hint of vulnerability. It had tempered the fire inside him.

He'd taken his hands off her arms and stepped back. 'What on earth are you doing?'

Apart from slowly driving me insane? He'd just managed not to utter that out loud.

But as he'd watched, he'd seen any hint of softness leave her face, to be replaced with something he recognised much more. A cool hauteur far more mature than her teenage years.

She'd shrugged a shoulder. 'I know you want

me, Vidi, and it's boring watching you try to resist.'

Vidi. She'd used to call him Vidi. As if they'd had that kind of relationship. As if they'd had any kind of relationship beyond the one in which she went out of her way to torture him.

He'd shaken his head, wondering why he'd ever thought he'd seen a chink of vulnerability. She was about as vulnerable as a tank.

'You are just a girl.'

Fire had lit her eyes, turning them even more golden. 'I'm eighteen today.'

In any other instance he would have wished her a happy birthday. But Eva was not someone he'd been able to behave rationally around.

Vidal had thought of how close he'd come to forgetting all of that at the feel of her body pressed to his, that provocative mouth moving so insistently under his. It had made him harsh. 'Go and find someone your own age to torture, Eva. I'm not available to be your plaything.'

Eva had lifted a hand, about to slap him across the face, when Vidal's lightning-fast reflexes snapped into action. He'd caught her wrist and held it tight, resisting the almost overwhelming urge to clamp his mouth to hers and show her exactly how thin his restraint was.

'Like I said, Eva…go and find someone your

own age to seduce. You are the last person I would ever touch.'

He'd dropped her wrist and turned and walked away, filled with more volatile emotion than he'd ever felt in his life. *She was dangerous.*

And now she was right in front of him, causing all those memories and sensations to swirl in his gut.

You came here, a voice reminded him, *because you're weak. Because you couldn't resist knowing if she's still the same. Or has she changed, softened?*

She *was* different, on first appearances, with her worn clothes and that haughty beauty that had matured into something far more potent.

But he suspected the differences were purely superficial. Underneath it all she was the same haughty entitled princess.

His eyes traced the dismayingly familiar lines of her face. Those huge wide-set golden-brown eyes. Strong dark brows. A straight nose. The high cheekbones showing her impeccable lineage. And that mouth… As full and provocative as it had been the last day they'd met but even more so now. Her skin was blemish-free and golden. Silky. Inviting him to touch.

His hand curled into a fist at his side. He said, 'Why am I here, Eva? Because I'm fulfilling my dying father's wishes and because I was curious.'

CHAPTER TWO

EVA SWALLOWED PAST a dry throat. 'Curious about what?' Her voice sounded croaky. She felt totally exposed, unprepared to see Vidal Suarez again.

He cast a look around the room, his hands back in his pockets, oozing insouciance. He might come from a humble background, but right now he looked far more entitled to be in this majestic space than her.

Was this what he wanted? To gloat at the tables being turned?

A sense of vulnerability made Eva voice that question out loud.

Vidal looked back at her. 'You really think I'm so petty or have the time to come here just so I can score a point?'

In Eva's world, with what she'd learnt from her mother, it was entirely feasible that he would want to do such a thing. She felt confused. 'Well…why, then?'

For a long moment it looked as if he had no

intention of telling her, but then he said, 'My father always loved this place and these gardens. Don't ask me why. I did not share his love.'

Me neither, thought Eva.

'When he was dying he said that he'd always wished my mother had been alive to see the gardens here, and that if I could do one thing for him it would be to save this place and rescue it from crumbling altogether. He knew that once he left there would be no one to tend to it.'

Eva shook her head. 'I can't believe it meant that much to him.'

'Because it means nothing to you. And yet you were born here? And your ancestors built it?'

Eva felt defensive. 'Just because I'm from this place, it does not mean that I have to love it. Is it so wrong to want to live my own life now?'

Vidal looked at her with narrowed eyes, making her feel even more defensive.

He said, 'Not at all. I can see how this place must have stifled you while your peers are living far more glamorous lives. No doubt you already have some hapless heir lined up in your sights, to transport you into a far more salubrious environment and lifestyle.'

For a second Eva thought she might actually laugh out loud. A sharp, semi-hysterical burst of laughter. And then she realised that Vidal Suarez had no idea about her life. He just assumed that because she came from this rarefied world it automatically gave her some kind of passport into a glittery existence. And that she wanted it.

It couldn't be further from the truth, and she'd known that for some time now. But, it was the life her mother had envisaged for her. To marry well and strategically. Her mother had wanted to show her errant husband that even though he'd rejected them, she could still make sure their daughter was accepted into society.

But it hadn't worked out like that. After years of being kept apart from society, when Eva had emerged she'd been woefully ill-equipped to fit into the crowd of her peers. On every level imaginable. She'd had none of the social skills or the knowledge she'd needed to navigate stepping into the fast-moving and cut-throat world of Spanish high society.

She recalled with burning mortification one party that her mother had managed—some-how—to get an invitation for. It had been the eighteenth birthday of one of the heirs of Spain's most elite family.

Having only recently turned eighteen herself, Eva had entered the exclusive hotel ballroom as shaky and nervous as a newborn foal, hating herself for it. The first thing she'd noticed with a wave of cold horror was that she was dressed in a fashion about a decade out of date. These people were sleek and sophisticated, even though they were still teenagers. She was overdone and too fussy. And then, as if they were one person, the entire crowd had seemed to turn to look at her. A hush had fallen over them and someone had sniggered.

Eva had fled to the nearest private space where she could hide. A toilet cubicle. Inevitably, she'd heard herself being discussed.

One girl had said to another in an awed tone, '*That's* Eva Flores? I thought she was an urban myth. How can a girl like us be hidden away for years like that?'

'Quite easily, obviously,' had come the dry response from her friend. 'I mean, did you *see* her? It's as if she's got stuck in a time warp. She's like one of those feral people found in the woods after being raised by wild animals. I don't think she's even wearing make-up!'

The girls had left the bathroom. Eva had crept out and found a discreet side entrance to escape through and had vowed never to go near one of those events again. And she hadn't.

Eva pushed down the toxic memories and cursed Vidal for bringing them back to life. 'What I plan to do in the future is no concern of yours. If you're not serious about purchasing the *castillo* then you can leave. I have engagements to keep.'

Like the one she had working as a chamber-maid in one of Madrid's most exclusive hotels. If she was late she didn't need to bother going in again—or so her boss had told her on her first day.

But she would die before she revealed that to Vidal. Bad enough that he thought her an impov-erished socialite. He didn't need to know the full grim reality. Even now, when her mother was dead and gone, Eva felt the strongly ingrained instinct to save face and not let Vidal see a mo-ment of weakness.

Vidal folded his arms. 'Oh, I'm serious about purchasing the property. I didn't come here for a reunion…as happy as this one is.'

The mocking tone surprised Eva. The Vidal she'd known before hadn't been a mocking per-son. He'd been serious. Most of the time. There had been one day when she'd been reading in her favourite private spot, seeking respite from her mother, when Vidal had appeared with some garden implements, obviously helping his father.

Even now Eva could recall the way her heart had skipped and then started beating again in a staccato rhythm. The way her skin had felt hot and how she'd been so aware of her skirt and short-sleeved top. Compared to Vidal, who'd been wearing a pair of board shorts and a worn T-shirt, she'd felt overdressed and totally uncool.

He'd stopped and looked at her over his sun-glasses, his mouth quirking slightly. 'Don't you ever meet other people?'

She'd felt acutely exposed. 'I don't need other people.' But the sad truth was that she'd had no friends.

'Everyone needs someone.'

'Did you read that on the back of a cereal packet?' she'd sniped back.

Vidal had just shaken his head, as if sad for her. 'You could smile once or twice, you know. It might actually entice someone to want to get to know you.'

He'd walked away and Eva's chest had felt so tight that it had hurt. In fact she'd always felt desperately lonely, for as long as she could re-member. She would have loved to have a friend. Pathetically, Vidal had been the closest thing she'd had to a friend, even though she hadn't been able to engage with him in a normal way. Her mother had made sure of that.

Her mother had used to whisper in her ear: *'You're better than everyone... Don't ever let a man think you want him, Eva... You are the prize, not them... You don't need anyone but yourself.'*

Except for this man, who had always made her feel as if he could see all the way under her skin to where she was so uncertain and needy and vulnerable.

It had taken the death of her mother for her to be fully released from the prison of believing she had to behave a certain way, and even now she found it difficult to trust her own instincts.

Eva forced the vulnerability out. There was too much at stake for her to wobble now. Vidal Suarez was just a man. He didn't possess magic powers. No matter what his various ex-lovers had breathlessly told the newspapers, creating quite the playboy mystique.

Moving towards the door leading into the reception area Eva said, 'Like I said, I have engagements. If you're serious about the property you have my solicitor's details. Feel free to look around and reacquaint yourself, but I'm afraid I have to leave.'

'What kind of engagements?'

Eva stopped and turned around. 'I have to meet some girlfriends for drinks.'

The minor lie was so much easier to say than the truth. The last thing she needed was to see pity on Vidal's face. She'd seen it before and she never wanted to see it again.

'I'm happy to hear you've made some friends.'

Eva's chest hurt. She still had no friends to speak of. Not really. One girl she worked with at the hotel was friendly, but Eva was conscious not to say too much for fear of her finding out that she was *Eva Flores*—an heiress who, improbably, had nothing to inherit, and who went home to an empty *castillo* every day. Would she even believe that Eva needed to work for minimum wage after the life she'd lived?

So, as nice as the girl was, and as friendly as they'd become superficially, Eva avoided all overtures to take it any further outside their work environment. She'd watch her colleague meet her boyfriend at the staff entrance and get on the back of his motorbike to go home and envied her life of freedom.

Eva needed to get away from Vidal now. He was too potent a reminder of everything she wanted to leave behind. Emotions were rushing to the surface and emotions were dangerous. Weakening.

'I have to go and get ready. You can let yourself out.'

'You're not worried about burglars?'

Eva cracked a tight smile. They'd sold off anything worth a cent in the last few years. 'No.'

She turned and walked out, aware of Vidal's gaze boring into her back. She couldn't believe that he had appeared here after all this time and was apparently serious about buying the property in his father's memory. Surely she should be the one feeling some ounce of sentiment and doing all in her power to cling onto her legacy?

You could go to your father, pointed out a voice.

Eva quashed it down straight away. She'd gone to him, begging for help, before her mother had died, and the way he'd treated her had told her in no uncertain terms that he was not an option. Never had been and never would be.

She was on her own, and if Vidal Suarez was going to be the one to help her get her freedom from the past then she had no choice but to accept it. But once the deal was done she would get on with her life and forget about his moment of gloating glory.

Vidal watched Eva walk out with all the grace of a prima ballerina. Even dressed down and against the backdrop of a crumbling *castillo*, she still exuded the nonchalance and the sense of entitlement of royalty.

He felt something drop inside him. Was it a sense of…disappointment? A sense of something slipping through his fingers? A slight lurch of panic that he might not see her again? But it couldn't be. Eva Flores meant nothing to him. He'd merely been curious as to the state of the *castillo* and to see if she was the same.

And now he'd satisfied his curiosity. In truth, the state of the *castillo* shocked him. He hadn't expected it to be so bad. He felt a prick of concern but quickly quashed it. Maybe some of Eva's bravado was gone, since her mother had died and she'd realised that she would have to sell her family's legacy to survive. But survive she would. Of that he had no doubt. She'd obviously been living here in her ivory tower until she could no longer deny the decay.

And now she was off to socialise with her peers and presumably find a suitable husband.

Vidal swept one last glance around the room. He didn't need to see the rest of the *castillo* to know it would be in a similar state. And he didn't need to be reminded of the poky apartment at the back of the *castillo* where he'd lived with his father. Treated like second-class citizens.

Only the fact that his father had expressed his wish for Vidal to do something about the *castillo* and its gardens had brought him here.

He'd always suspected his father had had a soft spot for Eva and her mother, in spite of the way they'd treated him. Vidal didn't understand it, but he didn't need to. He'd made up his mind about what to do with the *castillo* and once he had done the deal he wouldn't have to wonder about Eva Flores again. She would disappear into the society she'd been bred for and she was welcome to it.

Eva pushed her trolley down the hushed and quiet corridor. Luxurious carpet indicated that this was the VIP section of one of Madrid's most exclusive hotels and the décor was similar to what might be found in any royal palace.

This was her last turn-down service. Every bone was aching after hours of backbreaking work making beds and cleaning bathrooms. But it had helped to stop her thinking about what had happened earlier. With *him*. A man she'd never expected to see again and whom she was pretty sure had never wanted to see her again.

But now she couldn't stop thinking about it. And him. Was he really interested in buying the *castillo* or was it just some kind of elaborate wind-up just to inflict a little payback for her having treated him so badly in the past?

Somehow Eva didn't think Vidal Suarez was that petty. As he'd said, he had better things to do. Billions to accrue. Perhaps the story about his father was true and Mr Suarez really had loved the place. God knew, someone had needed to.

She shivered in the hotel corridor when she thought of the lingering sadness that permeated the *castillo*. Memories threatened to rise again, but Eva focused on the task at hand and gathered up the items she needed for the turn-down service.

She knocked lightly on the door of the biggest suite in the hotel. She wasn't expecting the guest to be present. At this time most guests were out or at dinner. So, without waiting for an answer, Eva said in a loud clear voice as she opened the door with her key, 'Good evening—turn-down service.'

But she came to an abrupt standstill in the doorway when she realised there was a man in the suite, approaching the door with a mobile phone held up to his ear. He saw her, and the shock she felt was mirrored on his face.

They said simultaneously, *'You.'*

Vidal Suarez spoke into the phone curtly. 'I'll call you back, Richard, there's someone at the door.'

Eva couldn't believe it. Vidal. Here. In this suite. Looking at her with unmitigated shock. The jacket, waistcoat and tie were gone. The top button of his shirt was open. It felt curiously intimate to see him like this.

Eva found her voice. It was flat. 'Turn-down service.'

'Is this before or after drinks with your girl-friends?'

'I lied.'

The speed with which she'd admitted that seemed to surprise him. He said, 'Why?'

Eva lifted her chin. She was still holding the turn-down service paraphernalia and standing in the doorway. Someone approached in the corridor. There was a woman's laughter. Soft and sexy. As if she was with a lover.

'Come in,' Vidal instructed, reaching past her to push the door closed before she could decide what to do.

Vidal walked into the vast, opulent suite. Eva had no choice but to follow. He turned to face her in the living area, coloured soft and golden by low lights. The city of Madrid twinkled beyond the windows.

'Why aren't you out?' Eva asked bluntly.

'I had remote meetings so I took them here. Why did you lie?'

Eva swallowed. She felt like squirming. 'Because I didn't want you to know how bad it is.' Or that she had no friends. *Still.*

Vidal frowned. 'Well, it's obvious there's not enough money left to keep the *castillo* intact, but is it worse than that?'

Eva nodded. Vidal's gaze dropped and she was suddenly very aware of her plain uniform of black button-down dress and apron. Hair scraped back. Tights. Flat shoes. Minimal make-up.

He reached towards her and said brusquely, 'Put those down.'

He took the things out of her arms and put them down on a nearby table. Now Eva felt even more exposed.

'How long have you been working here?' he asked.

'About a year.'

'Since your mother died.' It wasn't a question.

Eva nodded. 'We—that is, *I* have huge debts. Mother borrowed against the *castillo* to keep us afloat, to keep staff. Eventually we ran out of that too.'

'What about your father?'

Eva's father was from one of Spain's oldest family lines. She shook her head. 'Not an option.'

'That's not what it looked like in the press. I was in London too when you appeared beside him at that event.'

Oh, God. He'd been in the same city at the same time.

Eva felt a wash of shame rise up from her gullet. 'It wasn't what it looked like.'

She wasn't going to explain how her father had humiliated her that night, and had shown her the depth of his disregard for her.

Vidal made a sound that told Eva he doubted that, and turned away.

Normally when she came into this kind of suite she was on autopilot, wanting to get it cleaned and ready. It was quite different when she had a moment to take it in. Vidal looked as if he'd been born against this backdrop. The tables really had turned. Now she was the impoverished one. At his mercy. If he decided not to buy the *castillo*—

A flash of cold panic gripped her. She couldn't bear to be trapped there any longer. 'Are you going to buy the *castillo*?' The words were out before she could stop them.

Vidal was at the drinks cabinet. He turned around. 'Would you like something?'

Eva's throat was dry. 'Some water, please.'

Vidal smiled, but it was tight. 'Impeccably polite. You always had that quality at least.'

Eva's face burned. She was glad Vidal was facing away. Her gaze moved over his broad shoulders in the white shirt and down to where it was tucked into his trousers. Narrow hips. Long legs. Muscles moving under the thin material.

He turned around again and her gaze became locked on the middle of his chest. She could see the darkness of his skin under the material. The whorls of dark hair where his shirt was open at his throat.

He came towards her and handed her a crystal glass of sparkling water. She took a quick sip, and almost choked when it went down the wrong way. She'd never felt so gauche. And she'd been brought up to feel as if she was prepared, entitled to enter the most rarefied of spaces. But what she'd realised since her mother's death was just how woefully *un*prepared she was.

Her mother had lived in a dreamworld about two decades out of date. Oh, their name and lineage were still revered in some quarters, but the world had moved on, and scandal in the highest echelons of Spanish society had tarnished the respect they'd once held.

Not that Eva really cared about any of that. Her privilege had kept her apart from the world for too long. She longed for normality. To learn who she really was.

'Okay?' Vidal asked, bringing Eva back into the room.

She nodded. 'Fine.' She handed back the glass. 'I should get back to work. My manager will be looking for me.'

'You don't want to know my answer about buying the *castillo*?'

Eva went still. He was playing with her. She should have guessed. She felt the old familiar urge to hide behind the veneer she knew so well. 'I really couldn't care less, Vidal. If you don't, someone else will—eventually.'

Before Eva could stop him, he took her hands in his. The shock of physical contact rendered her mute. He held them and turned them over and back again. Suddenly Eva saw what he saw—the rough patches and dry spots. The short nails. Unvarnished.

He said, 'Oh, you care, I think. You weren't made for this.'

Eva pulled her hands back and put them behind her back. Struggling to focus on words that suddenly seemed elusive, she said, 'And yet here I am.'

He looked at her. 'Even dressed like this, and with raw hands, you can't disguise your nobility. That's quite a feat.'

Eva felt defensive and exposed. 'You've had your moment of karma, Vidal. I have to go.'

She turned to leave, but before she could get to the door Vidal said from behind her, 'Wait.'

Reluctantly, Eva turned around again. Vidal's face was in shadow, so she couldn't make out his expression, but for some reason her skin prickled. Not just with awareness, but with a sense of something about to happen.

Then he said, 'Actually, I have a proposition for you. It could solve all your problems—short-term and long-term.'

Eva frowned. 'What you do mean, short-term and long-term?'

'I'm talking about your debts and the *castillo* itself.'

He stepped into the light. She could see his expression now. Had it always been so unreadable?

No. He'd lost his layer of approachability. He was altogether a far more intimidating person.

'I told you it was a dying wish of my father's that I offer to do something with the place…?'

'So you said.'

'Well, as much as I loved my father, I'm not sentimental enough to spend a small fortune on a property that needs a mountain of work for little return. But I have devised a plan that could see it earn its own keep and potentially make a profit in years to come.'

Intrigued in spite of herself, Eva asked, 'How's that?'

'By turning it into an exclusive hotel and event space. The gardens alone, once restored, would be a huge draw. It's the ideal distance from Madrid. Guests could take a taxi into the city or enjoy the bucolic peace and quiet of the estate.'

Eva hadn't ever imagined what might happen to the *castillo*.

Vidal was looking at her carefully. 'It doesn't bother you? The plan I have?'

Eva shook her head. 'Should it?'

'Most people have an…attachment to their childhood home.'

Eva stiffened. She wasn't 'most people'. 'I don't care what happens to it. I just want it gone.'

'Well, that's contingent on one thing.'

'What thing?'

'If you do something for me, in return I will buy the *castillo*, settle all its debts and turn it into a profit-making enterprise. I will even offer you a stake, if you'd like.'

Eva couldn't quite compute this information for a long moment. She'd been facing the prospect of sizeable debts remaining even after the sale. But they would be gone. *And* he was offering her a business opportunity.

Then she recalled what he'd said and immediately she was suspicious. 'What do you want me to do for you?'

Vidal folded his arms. 'I want you to agree to a public engagement with me.'

Vidal watched Eva closely. Seeing her like this in a maid's uniform had thrown him. More than thrown him. He'd underestimated how impoverished she was. And yet not for a moment had she let that hauteur slip. As if he was the one doing her a favour by being available for a turn-down service.

Eva looked a little stunned. And then confused. 'A public engagement…like an event?'

'No. Like a marriage engagement.'

Eva went white. Something about her reaction made Vidal feel simultaneously insulted and vindicated by the impulsive decision he'd made.

'You want to marry me?' she asked, sounding shocked.

'Not in a million years,' Vidal responded. 'You're the last woman I'd ever want to marry.'

A little colour flared back into her cheeks and, perversely, it made him feel comforted. 'Why go through the charade of an engagement, then?'

'It would look good for me to appear more settled in the short term. I've cultivated a somewhat…lurid reputation in recent years, and it's affecting my business.'

'How?'

'I'm looking for investment in a new project. But I'm finding that the higher the stakes are, the more conservative the investors are. They're jittery. Not sure if they can trust me even though I've proved myself over and over again. You see, they can't quite pin me down. My background is not very palatable, and that makes them nervous too. On the social scene I now inhabit stability matters. Status matters.'

Eva spread her hands. 'How on earth can I be of any benefit?'

'You would add a certain…*authenticity* to my reputation. The elusive Eva Flores. Descended from one of Spain's oldest and noblest lines. Distantly related to royalty.'

Vidal wasn't sure what she muttered in response to that, but it sounded suspiciously like,

That's about all I'm worth. It hadn't been said with self-pity, though. More with a sense of anger.

'Your glittering social life obviously came to a standstill when your mother died,' he observed.

Eva realised that Vidal must be referring to the pictures he'd seen of her in London, when she'd gone to speak with her father. He obviously assumed that they reflected her life at the time. The reality couldn't be further from that impression. But she wasn't going to expose herself even more.

She still couldn't really wrap her head around what Vidal was proposing. She shook her head. 'Why would you want to do this with me?'

'As I said, by sheer dint of your birth, you have a status that I could never hope to attain. But by association...'

'Are you sure you want to be associated with someone who has fallen from grace?' Eva couldn't quite hide the brittleness in her voice.

'But that's it. You haven't been on the scene recently, so you bring no adverse baggage.'

'What about my parents? When my father abandoned us it caused quite a scandal.'

'They never divorced, though, so anything anyone might have said is just idle gossip.'

Just idle gossip. It had been the judgement of

their peers that had wounded her mother more than anything. The social ostracism. It would have almost been better if her father *had* divorced her mother, but he'd refused. Not wanting to lose any of his own money. Her mother had been too proud to pursue it. And Eva had always suspected that her mother had wanted her father to return. Even though theirs had been a very acrimonious relationship.

But that didn't seem to bother Vidal. Because for his purposes Eva still had value. In her name at the very least.

Enough value for a fake engagement to the one man on this planet who could look into her soul without even trying and lay her bare.

Eva's breath quickened at the thought of being literally laid bare in front of Vidal. It was the most terrifying thing she could think of. Terrifying and exhilarating. But mostly terrifying. Terrifying enough for her to resist.

'The *castillo* will sell eventually if you don't buy it.'

'It hasn't in a year. Are you prepared to wait another year?'

The thought of another year watching the *castillo* decay around her was enough to make Eva feel even more nauseous. But she hid it.

'If I have to.'

Vidal shook his head. 'Even now, when you

have nothing, your pride won't allow you to be seen with someone you consider inferior. I have to hand it to you—you're consistent at least. Your mother would be proud.'

It was safer for him to believe that she considered him inferior. It gave her a sense of armour.

Curious in spite of herself, she asked, 'How long would this be for?'

He shrugged minutely, as if he wasn't suggesting something totally audacious—asking her to pretend to be his fiancée.

'A month? Maybe two? That's all I need to secure a particular investment.'

Something about the way that he was being so cavalier with his pronouncements made Eva ask waspishly, 'Won't it look worse for you if you're only engaged for a brief time?'

Vidal shrugged. 'Once I get the investment I don't really care about people's opinions.'

'You used not to be so cynical.'

Vidal's face hardened. 'Life has made me cynical. And certain people in particular.'

Eva's heart thumped. 'You mean me?'

'Let's just say that you were my introduction.'

Eva knew it shouldn't hurt to hear him say that. But it did. The irony was that even though life had made her cynical too, she didn't want it. She hated it. And yet it was ingrained within her, and she didn't know if she'd ever be brave enough to be vulnerable or let it go.

Clearly what Vidal wanted here was a form of revenge, pure and simple. For the fact that she and her mother had never let him forget that he was beneath them. And her, primarily, for teasing him mercilessly and for punishing him when he'd rejected her. Humiliated her. Because when he'd walked away from her that day she'd known that she was the one who was lesser in every way.

She folded her arms over her chest. 'Isn't it kind of pathetic? Living out your father's dream to own the property where you both worked and then parade me on your arm like some kind of trophy?'

'It's no more pathetic than your teenage dream to seduce me.'

Eva flushed. 'I was bored.'

'You wanted me—and you still want me.'

You still want me.

The shock of his words landed in her gut like a punch.

'Don't be ridiculous...' she breathed. Terrified he would see that it wasn't ridiculous at all, she unfolded her arms. 'I don't have time for this— I'd prefer to take my chances. I need to get back to work.'

Sudden panic filled her, how long had she

been here? It felt like hours and it felt like a nanosecond.

'You go back to work and consider my offer. I'll be here until lunchtime tomorrow. You have until then to let me know that you've realised what I'm offering is your only option.'

Eva turned and walked back to the door.

From behind her she heard, 'Aren't you forgetting something?'

She stopped and looked back. Vidal was pointing at the turn-down things. There was the smallest glimmer of a smile playing around his mouth.

Anger at how easily he thought he could manipulate her made Eva say, 'Do your own turn-down service.' And she walked out, heart thumping so hard she felt almost dizzy.

If Vidal chose to make a complaint about her, she could get fired for this. She was an idiot to have let him get to her. But he'd always managed to get to her—from the moment she'd looked at him for the first time. Their eyes had locked and she'd felt as if he could see all the way into her, right down to where she locked away her most tender feelings, for fear that her mother would trample all over them.

And even though she only had herself to blame for behaving as she had around him, she'd always been hurt by his judgement of her—as if on some level she'd hoped that he could see through the armour she wore to the person underneath, who wasn't remotely spoiled or entitled. Who was, in fact, very lonely. And confused. And full of desires she didn't really understand.

Eva gripped the trolley and pushed it back down the corridor. There was no way she could agree to Vidal's shocking proposition. There was no way she could handle being in close proximity with him day after day. Not when he made her feel so exposed and called to the weakest part of her, where her desires threatened to overwhelm her and emotions swirled dangerously with too many memories to ignore.

She needed to escape the past, not return to it.

CHAPTER THREE

EVA COULDN'T SLEEP that night. In spite of everything she'd told herself, she couldn't stop the onslaught of memories. She wondered if she really had been that awful? To merit a level of antipathy where Vidal would have no problem using her to elevate his own standing?

Yes, said a voice.

There had been countless little aggressions. Some benign and annoying and others much more pointed. Like when he'd been studying for university exams during a holiday and he'd been lying outside, bare-chested and wearing board shorts.

Eva had been sent with a message from her mother, and she'd said officiously, while trying not to ogle his perfect body, 'Mother says you are not to lie about like some vagrant. This is not your home to do as you please.'

The words had turned to ash on Eva's tongue as Vidal had twisted to look up at her, making the muscles in his chest bunch and lengthen. She'd had an acute sense of floundering. Swimming far out of her depth.

'And what do *you* say, Eva?'

The sound of her name on his tongue had been deeply thrilling to her at seventeen years old.

'Have you got an original thought in your head?' he'd asked.

Eva had flushed, suddenly very conscious of her gangly limbs in culottes and a button-down shirt. She'd longed to be able to lounge around like him. His sense of ease had always fascinated her. His innate confidence. She'd felt prickly. Defensive. Aware that he was touching on something that was deeply disturbing—her mother's influence over her. But her mother was all she knew. Her only touchstone in this world.

She'd blurted out, 'What about *your* mother? Did she leave you and your father because you had nothing to offer her?'

Vidal had sprung to his feet so fast that she'd taken a startled step back. His face had gone white and he'd been livid. She'd never seen him look so intimidating.

'Do not *ever* mention my mother again.'

Eva had battled to overcome her sense of intimidation. She'd shrugged minutely. 'My father left too…it's not a big deal.'

Except of course it was. His abandonment

of Eva and her mother permeated the walls of this castle and every inch of its grounds like a toxic mist.

Vidal had gritted out, 'My mother did not leave us. She died.' And he'd gathered up his things and stalked off.

Eva had never seen him studying outside again.

Eva thumped the pillow under her head. But when she did finally fall asleep her dreams were no less disturbing than her memories. And when she woke in the morning the lingering tendrils of a vivid nightmare made her realise that maybe returning to the past was her only option. Maybe that was the only way to find her freedom.

That morning, Vidal looked at the dawn breaking over Madrid, bathing the city in a glorious halo of gold and pink. Grief clutched at his chest as he thought of his beloved father and mother. And how they had died so prematurely and never got to enjoy the fruits of his labour.

He often thought about the kind of house he would have bought them. The life of ease he would have given them after working so hard. His mother had been a seamstress, and one of Vidal's earliest memories was of the distinctive sound of her sewing machine. Day and night.

Soothing. But it had stopped when she'd died and everything had changed.

That was why he hadn't bought a property here yet—it felt wrong without them. His father had looked for a better job, having made a promise to his mother to ensure that Vidal had every opportunity to get to a decent school. She'd known Vidal had a prodigious talent.

Vidal's mother and father had had the kind of love and devotion that was rare. They'd never excluded Vidal either—their love had been big enough to encompass all three of them. And big enough to handle the fact that, after Vidal, his mother hadn't been able to have more children.

His experience of their love had given Vidal a lifelong ambition to replicate what his father and mother had had some day. He'd wanted someone as good and kind and selfless as his mother. He'd wanted that deep and pure connection. The kind of mutual support that was unspoken but stronger than steel.

But over the years he'd become cynical. The world he inhabited wasn't that simple. He'd realised how naive he was, how idealistic. The woman he wanted didn't exist. And yet he found himself clinging to the hope in spite of everything. Hoping that he might find that deep connection and love one day.

So why are you pursuing Eva Flores? asked a voice.

Vidal's mouth firmed. Because, as he'd told her, she was the one who had been his introduction to cynicism. So maybe she was the one who could help him exorcise it.

When he'd first met her he'd actually felt an affinity with her. They'd both lost a parent— her father wasn't dead, but he was gone—and they had no siblings. He'd thought they might be friends. But whenever he had reached out the hand of friendship, and whenever there might have even been a moment of communication, Eva would invariably say something or do something to remind Vidal of his place. Telling him he was not to fool himself into thinking he was her equal.

Even after he'd graduated from university and had begun making serious waves on the tech scene Eva had been coolly unimpressed. The most galling thing to remember now was that even though Vidal had no longer been under any obligation to go back and help his father during his holidays, he had *wanted* to go back. To see her. Endlessly fascinated in spite of himself. Fascinated to know if she was the same.

And each time she was. Only more beautiful and more haughty, if that was possible. As if maturity was only hardening her edges even more.

She was impermeable. And over the years any pity he might have had for her was eroded to nothing. She was born of a legacy and a society that he knew nothing about and wanted nothing to do with. It was in her bones and in her blood.

And yet now she's cleaning hotel rooms.

Vidal snorted to himself.

Only because she's too proud to let her peers see her so impoverished in public.

No doubt she had some plan, once the *castillo* was sold, to reintroduce herself to the society she'd had to hide from.

He was offering her a fast track to that end. So why wasn't she jumping at the opportunity?

Because it was with *him*. A nobody. Even if he did have billions now, he remained unpalatable to her.

The fact that he still wanted her was utterly galling. But he feared it was a hunger that would not go away until he'd had her.

You want to seduce her, insisted a little voice.

No, Vidal countered.

He was stronger than that.

But before he could stop it a fantasy emerged fully formed to mock him. A fantasy of making Eva come apart under his hands. Of all that haughty froideur melting, to reveal the flesh-and-blood woman underneath who couldn't deny that she was just that: flesh and blood.

He wanted to smash aside that ice and make her admit that he'd always driven her as crazy as she had him. He wanted it more than he needed her to help him secure any investment. And that revelation was enough to make him go cold. She still held him in the palm of her hand. She still mocked him for his weakness without saying a word.

As long as she existed in his fantasies like this he would not be able to move on. But he wanted more than this. He wanted a true connection. Love. And Eva Flores was the antithesis of that.

Coming here, indulging his curiosity, had been a weakness, exposing him. He'd become jaded. Time and experience had only sharpened his interest in what was forbidden. He shouldn't be surprised that Eva had managed to burrow under his skin again and lodge there like a sharp thorn. But it was time to let the fascination go. Her hold over him was illusory. He wasn't used to not having a woman he wanted. That was all. He'd wasted enough time on her.

He was done.

'I'm afraid Mr Suarez has checked out.'

'But it's only ten a.m.!'

Eva wasn't prepared for the sense of panic mixed with desolation that landed in her gut.

She said, 'He told me that he would be here till lunchtime.'

The concierge, who was new and didn't recognise Eva as being on the cleaning staff, said, 'He checked out last night. I'm sorry I can't give you any more information.'

Eva stepped back, conscious of the people behind her. She went and stood to one side, near a pillar, and tried to figure out what to do. She overheard two women talking nearby in not so quiet voices.

'Did you see her? I'm sure that was Eva Flores.'

'No way. No one has seen her in years. The girl is a ghost. She doesn't exist. You know her nickname was "the girl in the bubble", because she was only allowed out of that *castillo* about three times a year...'

Eva could almost hear the shudder in the voice of the other woman when she responded.

'That place is creepy. It looks haunted. She'll never sell it. She'll grow old there, like her mother. All alone and going mad.'

Eva couldn't breathe. It was as if they'd articulated the nightmare she'd had last night. Of growing old alone in the *castillo*. Bitter, like her mother. *Alone*. Trapped.

Even after she'd woken at dawn she hadn't been able to shake the awful clammy horror of that possibility in her future. So much so that she'd found herself deciding there and then that she would accept Vidal's offer and throw caution to the wind.

She wanted to live.

Maybe letting Vidal have his retribution was the only way of doing that.

So she'd come straight to the hotel and now he was gone. He hadn't even waited. Was he already bored toying with Eva?

She avoided the area where the two gossiping women were standing and went out of the hotel and rang her solicitor. He told her what she'd already feared: Vidal's people had called and said he was no longer interested in buying the *castillo*.

Eva felt sick. But she knew that she had only one option. She had to go and find Vidal and ask him to reconsider. Because he was the only thing that could stop her nightmare from coming true.

Vidal stood in the middle of a glittering crowd on the rooftop of one of London's most exclusive buildings. London was laid out before him in a carpet of lights, its tall buildings piercing the dusky sky. He was among some of the most important people in the country. In the world. Tech entrepreneurs like him. Moguls, models, actors, politicians... Even royalty.

He was a lot more comfortable in these sur-
roundings now, but sometimes he still felt like an
imposter. Impossible not to when most people in
this space had been born into privilege and took
it as their due. He was accepted—but only up to
a point. Some people still looked at him warily.

People like Eva.

He gritted his jaw. He hadn't been able to get
her out of his mind in the week since he'd left
Spain. Ridiculously, he was feeling guilty when
he thought of leaving her to her fate, when he
owed her nothing. Even worse was the frustration and irritation that she'd managed to leave
him feeling somehow at a loss. Exposed in his
desire for her.

Vidal finally responded to the incessant chat-
tering of a woman who was desperately trying to
get his attention and schooled his features into
some semblance of interest, when really his interest was back in Madrid.

So, when a movement out of the corner of
his eye made him look to his left, he thought
he was hallucinating. Eva Flores was just a
few feet away. Immediately standing out in the
crowd with her tall, willowy silhouette, wearing
a dusky pink wrap dress with one arm bared.
Hair pulled back. Minimal make-up. But she
didn't need make-up. Her bone structure alone
was enough to make people turn and stare.

He heard someone say, 'Who is *that*?'

For one cold, clammy moment he thought he really was hallucinating—that sexual frustration was infecting his mind. He blinked. No, she was still there. It was her. Unmistakably. And as that thought sank in and registered a sense of satisfaction settled deep in his gut. Along with something else he didn't want to acknowledge—*relief.*

Everyone else faded away. His eyes were locked with hers. Her chin had that little defiant tilt, as if to remind him that she was better than him. But she had come because she needed him too badly. Because she had a weakness too.

He'd seen her. So much for sneaking into this exclusive party and getting her bearings before Vidal noticed she was there. As soon as she'd walked in his head had come up, as if scenting prey, and he'd looked around and straight at her.

Nowhere to hide. She had to brazen it out now.

She walked towards Vidal and saw his eyes narrow on her. He wasn't wearing formal dress— a dark suit with a light shirt, open top button. No tie. She imagined how breathtaking he would be in a tuxedo.

She stopped a couple of feet away. She was vaguely aware of a woman beside Vidal emitting a huffy sound and flouncing away.

Vidal spoke first. 'Fancy meeting you here.'

Eva felt heat climb into her face. Vidal was looking at her with something distinctly…*satisfied* in his expression. She chafed against it, knowing that she'd had no other choice. That awful nightmare still lingered, even a week later.

She tried not to sound peevish, 'I went to the hotel the morning after we met, but you didn't even wait for my answer.'

'No, because I realised I'd wasted too much time in Madrid.'

Eva felt a sliver of panic. Perhaps even now it was too late?

She swallowed. 'Well, I wanted to talk to you.'

'Well, here I am.'

Eva looked around. She noticed people near them pretending to be studiously engaged elsewhere when they were clearly trying to eavesdrop.

She looked at Vidal. 'Could we talk somewhere a little less…public?'

'If you don't want to be seen with me in public then you shouldn't have come here.'

Eva frowned. 'I… No… That is, I didn't know where else to find you… I just feel it's too personal to discuss here.'

A waiter came by at that moment, with a tray full of glasses of champagne. Vidal took two glasses from the tray and handed one to Eva. 'Why don't you relax for a minute? You look tense.'

She felt tense. She clutched the glass in her

hand. She didn't want to be seen in public. She'd hated these kinds of situations ever since that hideously embarrassing event in Madrid when she was eighteen.

She'd sighed with relief when she'd stepped into this party and realised she'd got the tone right with the dress she'd hired from a designer shop here in London.

'You bring the glass to your mouth and you take a sip—like this…'

Eva's scattered attention was brought back to Vidal, who was taking a sip from the glass that looked impossibly delicate in his hand. Her eye followed the movement of his throat as he swallowed. Little flames danced across her skin, making it rise into goosebumps.

This was crazy. How could she hope to have a rational conversation with him when she was so aware of him and so wound up?

She took a sip and the sparkling drink danced down her throat, as if to mock her for being so serious. She tried consciously to relax, but social situations always made her nervous. She wasn't used to interacting with a large group of people. She'd never really been prepared for it—even though her mother had fully expected her to somehow charm and find a suitable husband after growing up in a bubble. Exactly as those women had said.

'When did you come over?' he asked.

'I came this morning.'

'Where are you staying?'

Oh, God, now Vidal was resorting to small talk. 'Um…a hotel near Piccadilly.'

Eva didn't want to admit that she was staying in a hostel near the train station, and that she had a flight booked to go home first thing in the morning. She'd changed in a bathroom at the hostel earlier, and had got some funny looks when she'd emerged, standing out amongst the backpacker tourists.

She scrabbled for something to say to avoid more questions. 'You look good here.' She stopped. Mortified.

Vidal arched a brow, amused. 'A compliment from Eva Flores? That is high praise indeed.'

Eva cursed herself. 'What I mean is that you… fit in. You've done well.'

Any hint of humour left Vidal's expression. 'For a kid from a minor suburb without a cent to his name and working-class parents?'

She looked at him. 'Well, that's the truth, isn't it? That's something to be proud of. What you've achieved is amazing.'

Yes, it was the truth. So why did her observation irritate him so much? Why was he suddenly so tense?

Because all he could see in his mind's eye was the tired faces of his parents and their red hands. Red from working.

And suddenly that sense of being an imposter was back, looming large over his shoulder. As if Eva's presence was all it had needed to re-emerge. Reminding him that he was only here through the sheer dumb luck of having a higher than average intellect and the ability to work hard.

He hated it that she pushed his buttons so easily. That she still had that power without even saying a word. Just by *being*.

It had been a mistake to think that she could bring something positive to his reputation. To his social standing. She'd done him a favour by turning up here to remind him of that.

But when Vidal opened his mouth to tell Eva that she was no longer welcome at this party, he found himself saying instead, 'Fine, let's go somewhere more private.'

Who was he kidding? His head didn't want Eva Flores anywhere near him, but his body was another matter, and right now his body was ruling his head.

'You don't have to leave. I don't mind waiting.'

They were standing at the elevator. Vidal didn't respond. Eva was desperately trying to maintain her composure, but it was hard when Vidal's hand was big and cupping her elbow. Skin to skin.

The elevator doors opened, and when they stepped in an attendant pressed the ground-floor button. The space was too small. All Eva could smell was Vidal. Sharp and spicy and masculine.

She said, a little threadily, 'You can let me go now.'

Vidal looked down, as if surprised that he was holding on to her. He didn't let go straight away, though. He took his time. Fingers trailing over her skin, leaving goosebumps behind.

Finally, Eva felt as if she could breathe again. The elevator doors opened onto the lobby of what was one of London's most exclusive hotels. Luckily, Vidal's social activities were well documented in the press, so she'd found out about this party relatively easily.

She could have tried to meet him at his London office once she'd found out he was here for the week, but the thought of being refused entry had been daunting. So she'd figured a social event might be easier. And it had been. Until now.

They were outside the building and a sleek SUV with tinted windows was waiting. The driver got out and opened the back door. Vidal extended an arm to Eva. 'Please…'

She didn't move. 'Where are we going?'

'To my apartment. It's not far from here.'

The thought of being alone with Vidal made her feel nervous and excited all at once. 'Can't we just go somewhere like a quiet bar?'

Vidal's jaw hardened. 'Do you want to talk or not?'

Of course she did. That was why she'd come here.

Reluctantly she moved forward and sat into the back of the car. The driver closed the door and Vidal got in on the other side, immediately dwarfing the cavernous space.

The vehicle moved smoothly into the London traffic, barely making a sound. An electric car. They didn't speak on the short journey. The car stopped outside a tall, sleek-looking apartment building. A concierge greeted Vidal and then they were in another elevator, and Eva's stomach swooped as they moved smoothly skyward.

The doors opened, and it was only when they opened directly into an apartment that she realised it had been a private lift. The apartment was breathtaking. Contrary to what Vidal probably thought, Eva really hadn't ever been anywhere like it.

Dark, moody tones were lightened by floor-to-ceiling windows showcasing a glittering view of the London skyline. Massive paintings were hung on the walls, and comfortable couches and chairs were dotted artfully around the space, with coffee tables groaning under big hardback books on photography and art.

Low lamps sent out seductive pools of golden light. It was a far cry from the spartan apartment Vidal and his father had once shared at the *castillo*.

Eva was rooted to the spot beside the elevator doors, which slid closed behind her with a muted *swish*.

Vidal had walked into the apartment, not even checking to see if Eva was following him. He was slipping off his jacket and draping it casually over the back of a chair, heading to what looked like a drinks cabinet.

He said over his shoulder, 'Can I offer you a drink?'

Eva felt so tense she thought she might crack. Maybe a drink would help her feel marginally more relaxed. She'd barely touched the champagne at the party.

'Sure, maybe a small white wine?'

He mixed a drink for himself and duly came back to her with a glass of perfectly chilled white wine. She took a sip quickly, and then saw Vidal hold his own tumbler up and say with a mocking tone, 'Cheers...'

Eva felt very unsophisticated. Sheepishly, she echoed, 'Cheers.'

'Please, make yourself comfortable.' Vidal waved a hand to indicate the vast expanse of his lounge area.

The sheer amount of choice made Eva move instead towards one of the windows. London twinkled and glittered under a clear sky. Helicopters traversed the city with blinking lights.

She was very conscious of Vidal behind her. Watching her. Waiting for her to beg for mercy. For a handout. For help. For her life.

She steeled herself and turned around. 'Look, Vidal, it's obvious you've decided to change your mind about the *castillo* and the...' She trailed off.

'The fake engagement?' he supplied helpfully.

'Why?' she asked hoping she didn't sound too needy. Or desperate.

He came and stood at the window, tumbler in his hand. He said, 'It was a moment of weakness to even want to see you again. See what you might have become. See if you had changed at all.' He looked at her. 'I don't indulge in weaknesses. But you always pushed my buttons, Eva.'

Her insides swooped and dived. 'I was young...'

Vidal looked back out of the window and made a dissenting sound. 'Yet you knew how to patronise those around you before most people could even spell the word.'

Eva swallowed her defence. How could she even begin to articulate what she had only come to terms with in the past year—the depth of her mother's malign influence on her life?

Desperately, she cast around for another way to try and get through to Vidal. 'You said it was your father's dying wish that you do something to restore the *castillo*…'

He responded easily. 'I also said I wasn't sentimental. My father was raving at the end…high on morphine. He thought he saw my dead mother standing behind me in the room.'

Eva had never known Vidal could be so obdurate. Feeling a sense of futility, she looked blindly at the view. 'Your father felt sorry for me, you know.'

'I know.'

'He used to say to me that there was a whole world outside the *castillo* and I had to get out and explore it…find my own way.'

'So why didn't you?'

'It wasn't that easy. My mother became unwell. I had to care for her.'

'And now you've lost precious time in establishing yourself on the scene, and perhaps no one is really that interested in an heiress with nothing but a pile of medieval bricks to her name?'

Eva forced a tight smile. 'You have it all worked out.'

'Because, let's face it, it's not as if you're qualified to do anything else.'

Eva realised this wasn't going anywhere, and she was terrified that the longer she stayed the more likely it would be that Vidal would notice her awareness of him. An awareness that she couldn't hide.

She set her glass of wine on a nearby table. She hadn't even put down her clutch bag. It was still clamped in her other hand. 'I think it's best if we stop wasting each other's time. You should go back to your party, Vidal.'

She forced herself to look at him. His face was cast in shadow as he turned to face her from the window. The glow of the city outside made the lines on it look grim. She sensed he was fighting some kind of inner battle, but she needed to move on and try and seek salvation elsewhere.

'It was nice to see you again…and I'm happy that you are doing so well.'

'Are you, Eva? Really happy? Because you don't look it.'

That nearly felled her. *Happy.* The fact that he'd noticed she wasn't. Her chest felt tight. *Dios.*

'I'm perfectly fine, Vidal. Thank you for your concern. Now, I should go.'

She turned and took a step towards the door,

which felt very far away, across an expanse of luxurious carpet.

Vidal said, 'Back to work at the hotel tomorrow?'

Eva stopped. Turned around again. A spurt of anger mercifully diluted her emotion. 'Are you intent on torturing me until the last moment, Vidal? It's not enough to dangle the solution to all my problems under my nose and then whip it away at the last minute? I think you've made your point now—your life was a misery while you were at the *castillo* and now you're wreaking your revenge.'

Vidal stepped out of the shadows. He put his glass down on a table. He shook his head. 'It wasn't a misery, actually. My father enjoyed working there and I enjoyed helping him. It just got miserable when we had to deal with your mother—or when you decided that *that* day would be a good day to subject me to a little torture.'

Eva's heart thumped. She'd never known she'd had such an effect on him. 'Torture? That's a strong word.'

'It felt like torture. Being so aware of you and being so aware that everything about you was forbidden. Your age, your experience, your social status... All far beyond my reach. And yet that didn't stop you from parading yourself in front of me at any opportunity, looking for attention.'

Eva longed to defend herself. She hadn't known what she was doing. She'd had no idea of her effect on Vidal. She'd only known of his on her. She said, almost accusingly, 'I could say the same of you.'

He frowned. 'What are you talking about?'

Eva cursed her runaway mouth. 'The midnight swims you took. *Naked.* You knew where my room was. You knew I'd hear you.'

A vivid memory sprang fully formed into her head before she could stop it. Late one night, under a full moon, Vidal hauling himself out of the pool in one graceful move, muscles flexing and bunching. Water sluicing down over perfectly sculpted muscles. His back broad, waist narrow. Buttocks muscular. And then he'd turned around, as if aware he was being watched. And Eva's avid gaze had dropped to the dark hair between his legs where, even after a cold swim, he'd been impressive.

He'd looked like a Greek statue. The embodiment of physical perfection. And then he'd looked up and their eyes had met. And Eva had stepped backwards so rapidly she'd tripped and fallen over. Pulse hammering. Feeling like an idiot. Completely exposed because she'd known he'd seen her.

'In case I need to remind you, that was the only time I *could* swim, as your mother had forbidden use of the pool for employees and their families. Not that she ever used it herself. You did, though.'

Yes, she had. And all her raging teenage hormones had been channelled into testing and pushing the boundaries of her newly forming sexuality and provoking a reaction from Vidal.

The days he'd been around had been heady. The days when he hadn't had felt cold, as if the sun had dipped behind a dark cloud. She'd come alive when he'd been at the *castillo*, and the memory mocked her now.

She must have been so obvious and gauche. He'd already been a man of the world, and because of the narrative her mother had fed her Eva had somehow believed that she was as sophisticated as the women he was meeting in America. When in fact she hadn't even been kissed! Which was what had led her to make that audacious move on her eighteenth birthday…which had ended in humiliation and disaster.

How Vidal would laugh at her if he even had an inkling that nothing had changed for Eva since that day. She was as innocent as ever. As unworldly. Except he appeared to believe that up until her mother's death she'd generally been living the high life.

She lifted her chin. 'We can keep going around like this in circles, Vidal, but ultimately we're going nowhere.'

'Do you know what that does to me?'

'What?'

'When you lift your chin like that?'

'Like what?'

'Like *that*. You're doing it now and you don't even notice.'

'What does it do to you?'

'It makes me a little crazy.'

'In what way?'

'You're pretending you don't feel it too?'

Eva's heart palpitated. Surely he couldn't mean…? 'I don't know what you're talking about.'

Vidal gave a short, curt laugh. 'Because I'm still the last man you would admit to wanting when we're not within the grounds of the *castillo*?'

'That was a long time ago…' breathed Eva, horrified that he was mentioning what had happened. Horrified that he remembered. 'It was nothing…a silly moment.'

'It didn't feel stilly. It felt very serious. I can still remember how you trembled against me.'

'Stop it.'

Eva's jaw was so tight it hurt. Not content with

teasing her with an offer to buy the *castillo*, now he was intent on humiliating her. Again.

'Do you know why I remember?'

'I don't care.'

'Because I haven't been able to get that moment out of my head—or the countless other moments when you intended me to notice you. The inconvenient truth is that I want you, Eva Flores.'

CHAPTER FOUR

EVA HEARD VIDAL say the words but they wouldn't go into her brain. They were in her body. That was where they impacted. Right in her solar plexus. She couldn't breathe. Her pulse was tripping. The tiny hairs were lifting all over her skin. And deep inside, where she hid her innermost secrets and insecurities and vulnerabilities, a pulse throbbed and heat flowed. Melting. Exposing. *Weak.*

'That's not true…' she breathed.

Vidal nodded his head. 'It is. And you want me too.'

She was dizzy. Was it that obvious? Feeling desperate, she said, 'You're the last man on earth I'd want.'

He took a step towards her and she almost stumbled backwards, filled with a mixture of adrenalin, panic, and something far more disturbing.

He said, 'You've wanted me from the moment you saw me, in spite of my status.'

She couldn't lie. Not here, under that gaze. 'Maybe I did…a long time ago. A teenage crush.'

'Pretty strong crush. You kissed me. And when I didn't kiss you back you—'

'You didn't want me then.' She cut him off, not wanting to hear him say what she had almost done in a fit of thwarted passion.

Vidal's eyes darkened. 'Oh, I wanted you. But you weren't ready.'

'And now I am?'

'You're a grown woman, aren't you?'

What he meant by that was that he assumed she was experienced. The thought of him finding out that she was as inexperienced as she'd been all those years ago made her feel nauseous.

She feigned bravado. 'Of course.' And then, 'But what does this have to do with…anything?'

'I've decided that my offer is still open. To buy the *castillo*, settle your debts, and even give you a stake in the business.'

'In return for…?'

'Standing by my side and looking suitably devoted when I announce our engagement.'

'A fake engagement.'

'Of course. I have no intention of marrying you.'

This was said with such assurance that Eva

found herself asking, 'But you do intend to marry?'

'Absolutely. Some day. To a woman I can love and respect.'

This caught at Eva on many different levels. Too many to pick apart now. Her chief emotion was hurt, when he shouldn't be touching on her emotions at all.

A little waspishly, she said, 'Then why put yourself through being anywhere near me at all?'

'Because I want you. And because I know I won't get you out of my mind until I've had you.'

Until I've had you.

Something about the crudeness of his language thrilled Eva even as it horrified her. And then she realised that he'd admitted that she'd been on his mind. But somehow it didn't make him seem weak, which was what she might have expected if she'd made such an admission.

'You're saying I'd have to sleep with you?' Eva was glad her voice sounded suitably affronted when inwardly she was slowly going on fire.

'No, I didn't say you'd have to sleep with me. I said that I want you. I am not in the habit of forcing women to sleep with me.'

Eva felt confused. 'But then...if I don't sleep with you...would we still have a deal?'

'Oh, you'll sleep with me—and it'll be entirely of your own volition.'

Her pulse thundered. 'You're very sure of yourself.'

Vidal shrugged minutely but didn't say anything else. He didn't have to. It vibrated between them. This awareness. This *heat*.

It's not going to happen, Eva promised herself.

Being so aware of Vidal and being forbidden to do anything about it was like an ink stain on her skin…she'd worn it for so long.

Apart from that one time when she'd tried to kiss him. And he'd humiliated her, exactly as her mother had warned her would happen if she let herself show any weakness.

She was older now. And, while she wasn't more experienced, she wasn't given to moments of exposing herself with unrestrained passion. This Vidal was infinitely more intimidating. It would be easy to resist him.

She didn't fear that he would coerce her. He was too proud. He'd always had the kind of innate pride that she'd never really had, in spite of her mother's insistence that she had every reason to be proud.

Vidal looked at her. 'Well? What's it to be, Eva? Because either you stay here now or you go, and if you go this time I promise you that we will never see each other again.'

Ridiculous to feel such a lurch of emotion at that thought. Either way, even if she agreed, she would never see Vidal again once they were done. It was abundantly clear that he hated himself for wanting her. And perhaps that would make this easier—it wasn't as if he was even pretending to like her. To charm her. What must it be like to be someone he desired and didn't resent desiring? The thought was provocative.

She felt as if she was taking a leap into a void, but at the same time she had no choice. 'I… Okay, yes, I'll stay.'

There was a pregnant pause during which Vidal didn't respond, and for a horrifying moment Eva thought he was going to tell her that it was all a joke and of course he wasn't going to go through with the deal.

But then he became brisk and said, 'I'll get you a pen and paper. Write down the name of your hotel and room number and I'll have my driver pick up your things. I'll show you around and then you can rest. We can discuss further plans in the morning.'

Eva didn't know what to say, so she just took the pen and paper from Vidal and wrote down the details.

He gave her a quick impersonal tour of the impressive apartment, with its state-of-the-art kitchen, two dining rooms—one formal—and the formal lounge they'd just been in. There was also a less formal one, with soft couches, books on shelves and a media centre.

When he showed her into a spacious suite with its own bathroom, dressing room and sitting room, which clearly wasn't his space, she realised that he wasn't expecting her to fall into his bed that night. She felt very gauche, and also, bizarrely, a little dizzy with how fast this was all happening.

Vidal stood in the doorway and Eva felt the chasm between them. A chasm that she had put there from the first day they'd met. A chasm nurtured and supervised by her mother, for fear that Eva might forget for a minute who she was and speak to Vidal as if he was her equal.

She felt a little lost and hated herself for it.

Before she could say anything, he spoke. 'You know where everything is now. Please make yourself at home and help yourself to anything you'd like. The kitchen is well stocked.'

And then he was gone. The door shut behind him.

Eva sat down on the edge of the bed. For the first time in days…months…even though she was in an environment that was more hostile than friendly, she felt a sense of relief wash over her.

If she could just resist Vidal, and if she could weather the public scrutiny of being by his side as his fake fiancée, then she would emerge with her whole life ahead of her. Free from the past once and for all.

What the hell are you doing, man?

The question resounded in Vidal's head as he stood at his office window, looking out over the city. His driver had just returned with Eva's bag. A small case. It had once been very expensive, but now it was battered and falling apart.

Like the castillo.

Also, his driver had informed him that she hadn't been checked into a hotel—the address had been for a hostel, near the train station.

So what? he asked himself. So she was proud and hadn't wanted him to know the extent of what she couldn't afford? He could have figured that out from the fact that she was working as a chambermaid in a hotel.

Earlier, he'd told himself he wanted nothing to do with her—and seeing her at the party had confirmed that for him. He'd made the right decision in deciding to cut all ties—leave her to her fate. After all, he owed her nothing. And yet he'd invited her back to his apartment. Because the truth was that he couldn't let her walk away. He might have temporarily fooled himself into thinking he didn't want her, or that his desire would fade, but seeing her here, on his turf, in that dress…all bets were off now. There was no turning back.

Interestingly, she hadn't behaved as he would have expected in his apartment. She'd looked uncertain. Awed. She'd gone to stand at the window and looked out as if she'd never seen such a view before. And then he'd cursed himself. Of course she had—she'd been here before. He'd seen those pictures of her in London, wearing a dress that had barely been modest. Surrounded by equally scantily clad women. Champagne flowing. Men leering.

That lifestyle had only stopped when she'd had to take responsibility for the *castillo* on her mother's death, and she must have resented it so much.

She was just toying with him. Pretending to be in awe. Amusing herself, no doubt. Waiting for him to patronise her so that she could remind him of who she was.

If that was the case, why did it still bother him? He was immune to Eva's games now. *He* would be the one in control this time, manipulating events to suit himself.

He would make the most of her presence by his side to be accepted professionally, in a way that had eluded him up to now.

Once he'd made headlines because of how he'd pulled himself out of the margins of society. Now those same newspapers speculated as to who his parents had been, and just *how* he'd really got those scholarships.

As much as people loved a rags-to-riches story, once you were in the *riches*, and mingling amongst the great and good, it became a different story.

After his father had died, he had gone through a crisis of sorts. Grief for his father, old grief for his mother, and lamenting that he couldn't share his wealth with them had driven him on a hedonistic spiral of wanting to forget the pain for a while.

He'd given himself over to a time of finding transient pleasures, earning himself a reputation as a playboy. People had started whispering things like, *'Well, it's no wonder...look at where he came from... He can't take his success seriously...'*

And that was when his business had started to suffer.

But he'd spent too many years working and sweating to be accepted to fall at the final hurdle. The final hurdle being the fact that no matter how much money or success he had, he needed to prove that he was worthy.

Eva, even with her vastly diminished finances and the fact that her parents had separated all those years ago, was still that exclusive and invisible invitation into a privileged world.

So, no. He hadn't made a mistake in changing his mind. He would improve his reputation by association and by appearing more settled. And if she was using him just to get a step back into her own world then what of it? What did he care where she went or what she did when he was done with her? She would be welcome to return to her peers...to find a suitable husband among the pure bloodlines of Spain's great families.

Out of nowhere an image sprang into Vidal's head of Eva with a dark-haired child in her arms. Smiling, playing, laughing. Before he could stop it, it caught at his gut like a vice. He crushed it. That image was a total fantasy, because Eva Flores didn't have a maternal bone in her body. How could she when he'd never seen her display an ounce of compassion or kindness?

There was no fear of his emotions being involved where Eva Flores was concerned. She was the last woman on the planet he could love. She epitomised everything he didn't want in a partner. She was cold, aloof and supercilious. She was rude and mocking.

But right now she was the only woman he wanted, and his desire burned him. Women didn't ever take up his mental energy like this. He wanted them, he had them, he moved on. She was no different.

Eva woke when the light of the rising sun moved across her face the following morning. She hadn't pulled the curtains closed last night. She realised she was on top of the bed covers and still in the robe she'd found on the back of the bathroom door, after having a long hot shower.

When she'd emerged from the shower she'd seen that someone had delivered her bag and left it just inside the door of the bedroom. Vidal? Her heart had thumped as she'd thought of him coming into the room while she'd been naked in the shower…

She'd slept surprisingly well, considering the circumstances.

She wasn't going back to Spain in the immediate future. She would have to call the hotel. Leave her job. Not that they'd miss her. They had a huge staff turnover. Working there had given her huge respect for all the invisible workers who came and went at dawn and dusk to cater for people like her, who would never have noticed them before.

In fact, her whole experience since her mother had become ill and she'd had to care for her had been a huge eye-opener—and not an unwelcome one. She'd realised how insular her life had been with her mother, and how…rarefied.

She'd gone to a private prep school with other children until she was twelve, and there she had had some friends. But it was as if that had been a turning point, and her mother had taken some kind of a paranoid turn. When Eva had been due to go to secondary school her mother had insisted on her staying at home and being privately tutored. Her mother had wanted to keep Eva apart, as if she was keeping her away from bad influences. Or *any* influences.

Eva had seen her friends from time to time, but gradually she'd realised she was losing touch with their lives. She hadn't been able to keep up with the references they made, and she'd soon stopped being asked to meet them or go to parties. She'd become uncool. Unwanted. And her life had slowly closed in on itself.

Until Vidal had arrived with his father, and Eva's world had exploded into sensations and cravings and emotions that she'd struggled to hide. Emotions that he still affected and that she still had to do her best to hide.

Eva got up and washed and dressed in the casual clothes in her bag. Jeans and a plain white shirt. Sneakers. She pulled her hair back into a low bun and took a breath before leaving the bedroom. Vidal had always been up at the crack of dawn, and things didn't appear to have changed when she found him sitting in the informal dining room by the kitchen.

She was startled when a woman came out, dressed in a uniform. Middle-aged, friendly. She was carrying a coffee pot.

'Coffee is fresh, Miss Flores. Help yourself

to anything on the table, or I can make you a cooked breakfast if you'd like?'

Eva shook her head. 'No, thank you, that won't be necessary.'

The table was full of an array of fruit, granola, yoghurts, pastries. She was avoiding looking at Vidal, of course. She'd seen enough of him to know he was dressed in dark trousers and a light blue shirt. Open at his throat.

She sat down at Vidal's right, and the housekeeper poured her some coffee. Eva thanked her. When she'd gone back into the kitchen Eva looked at Vidal, who was watching her. She felt her skin heat and took a quick sip of coffee, wincing slightly.

'It's hot,' Vidal said, a little redundantly.

Eva put down the cup. 'It's good.'

'You slept well?'

Eva reached for some fruit and granola. 'Yes, thank you. The bedroom is very comfortable.'

'Yes, it is. The apartment is a good base for London.'

'You own it?'

'I own the building. My London offices are a few floors down.'

Eva nearly choked on a piece of apple, but managed to swallow it before she embarrassed herself by telling him he'd done well again. He wouldn't take it as it was meant. He'd think she was patronising him.

Thankfully they were interrupted by the housekeeper. 'That'll be me, then, Mr Suarez—unless you need anything else?'

He smiled at the woman and Eva was mesmerised. It transformed his face and reminded her of when he'd been much younger. Less stern. More open.

'That's all, thanks, Mrs Carter. We'll be heading to the States later today, so I'll have my assistant let you know when we're due back. Probably not for at least a couple of weeks.'

The woman nodded and smiled at Eva. 'Goodbye, Miss Flores, I hope you enjoy your trip.'

And then she was gone.

Eva's head was buzzing with questions. 'Who is *we*…? And the States? As in America?'

Vidal said, '"We" is you and me—and, yes, America. That's where I'm based now. In San Francisco. That's where I consider home. London is just my European base.'

Eva absorbed this and felt a spurt of anger. 'I know I've more or less signed myself over to you for this…this fake engagement, but when were you going to inform me about this? And why didn't you introduce me to your housekeeper?'

'I was going to inform you. And I didn't introduce you because I didn't think you would care to be introduced. You never seemed inclined to care much about the staff before.'

Eva was speechless with indignation. But then she realised he had a point. Her mother hadn't liked her to address the staff beyond what was strictly necessary. Even the few staff they'd had left towards the end.

Eva felt piqued. 'Well, for future reference, you can introduce me to whoever is working for you.'

'Making beds and cleaning bathrooms has had an effect on you.' Vidal's tone was dry.

Eva felt like sticking her tongue out at him, but resisted the urge.

He stood up. 'I have a couple of calls to make in my study, but come in in about fifteen minutes and I'll fill you in on the plans.'

The plans. The plans to pretend to be engaged? The plans to share his bed?

Eva went hot and then cold when she thought of Vidal realising how innocent she still was. He *couldn't* find out.

When Vidal had gone, she finished her breakfast and coffee, waited the fifteen minutes, and then went to Vidal's study and knocked on the door.

'Come in.'

Had his voice always been so deep? It seemed to resonate right through her body.

She pushed the door open into a surprisingly

bright and modern space, painted light grey, with floor-to-ceiling shelves full of books and another massive window showcasing the spectacular view. Vidal was behind a huge desk with three computers, a laptop, and various other bits of tech equipment.

'Come in…sit down.'

Eva felt as if she was there for an interview.

She sat down on the other side of the desk.

Vidal shut his laptop. 'The reason we're going to San Francisco today is because the investors I'm trying to engage with are due to attend a series of events there over the next couple of weeks. It's too good an opportunity to miss, and the perfect place for us to start appearing as a couple,' he said. 'I had hoped to go back to Spain, to let you gather anything you needed from the *castillo* and tie up some loose ends, but we won't have time now.'

'Oh… I hadn't expected that. I can call my job from here, and there's nothing in the *castillo* that I really need.'

'Clothes?'

Eva thought of all the vintage designer dresses belonging to her mother, which she'd had to sell off to make some money. And then of her own very paltry clothes. Ever since her humiliation at that society birthday party she hadn't trusted her own judgement when it came to clothes—and anyway, she hadn't had the money to buy any.

'There's nothing there for me to pick up,' she said, and then she remembered something. 'Actually, that dress I was wearing last night…it needs to be returned to the hire shop.'

'You *hired* the dress?'

'I can't afford a dress like that.'

Vidal made a note on a pad. 'I'll have my assistant pay them for it—you can keep it. And we'll need to get you more clothes. I'll have a stylist meet us when we get to San Francisco. We'll announce the engagement ASAP.'

To avoid thinking about standing beside Vidal in public and pretending to look besotted, Eva said, 'Who are these investors you need so badly?'

Vidal stood up and went to the window, giving Eva a view of his broad back tapering down to slim hips and the muscular globes of his bottom. Long legs… He was more like an athlete in his prime than a tech nerd.

He turned around and Eva lifted her gaze, but not before she caught the look in Vidal's eye. He knew she'd been checking him out. Damn him.

He said, 'They're people who are very instrumental in the industry—the original disruptors. They have access to the kind of funding that just doesn't exist anywhere else, and the project I'm working on needs the funding they can give.'

'Why are they reluctant to invest? Surely you've proved your track record by now?'

'Because they've become more conservative, and they think that while my business is solid, my personal…volatility is detrimental to their reputation.'

Eva frowned. 'But that's silly. Either your work speaks for itself or it doesn't.'

Vidal's mouth twitched. 'Very noble—and spoken by one who comes from a world where you are trusted and granted access purely because of your name.'

Eva's chin lifted and she didn't even care. 'I didn't know you had such a chip on your shoulder.'

Vidal's mouth turned serious. 'I used not to—until I realised that, much as I'd like to believe otherwise, name and legacy still have a powerful sway. Along with reputation. Especially when millions of dollars are involved.'

Eva bit her lip. 'Do you really think it'll help, having me by your side? Most people over there won't have ever heard of me.'

'They'll find out.'

'Then they'll find out that my parents were separated.'

Vidal waved a hand. 'That's not a big deal. What's more important is that you come from old money and a distinct lineage.'

'You mean *no* money,' Eva muttered.

'Your father still has money.'

She looked at him and tried to hide her sense of hurt and abandonment. 'Really? I wouldn't know.'

'Well, it's obvious that he isn't helping you out.'

'My mother and I didn't see a cent of his money from the moment he walked out of the *castillo*. If the *castillo* hadn't been hers by inheritance from her parents, he would have probably tried to take that too.'

Vidal looked at her. 'So what were you doing with him in London?'

Eva stood up, agitated. 'I don't really think that's relevant right now.'

'You said before that it wasn't how it looked. Tell me how it was.'

'What do you care?'

'Humour me.'

Eva started to pace back and forth, folding her arms across her chest. She turned to Vidal. 'Don't you have things to do before leaving?'

'No rush—private plane.'

Of course. She should have known. She glared at him, hating him for pushing her on this. It was too huge, too humiliating. She couldn't bear to expose herself here…now. Not when Vidal was so remote. Stern. He wouldn't understand.

So she schooled her features, hid her emotion and shrugged minutely. 'It was exactly what you saw—a party. My father just happened to be there too. I partied for a few days…went shopping…and then I went home. That was it.'

Vidal looked sceptical. Eva didn't care. He'd already seen too much. He couldn't ever know the full extent of what had happened that night. It was too painful.

To her relief, he appeared to let it go. He said, 'I need to go down to my offices for an hour or so, to meet with my team and make arrangements. Give me the details of the dress-hire shop and write down your measurements.'

Eva did as he asked and handed him the piece of paper.

He said, 'Pack up your stuff and be ready to go when I get back.'

'I'm already ready.' Because she literally had nothing with her.

Vidal said, 'Good.' And then he left.

Eva congratulated herself on not letting him see into her too deeply. And then she realised that she would have to keep up this level of self-defence for the next month…two months?

Suddenly that felt more daunting than anything else she'd ever done in her life.

CHAPTER FIVE

'YOU'VE NEVER BEEN on a private plane before? I find that hard to believe.'

Eva sent a scowl towards Vidal. 'What part of asset-rich, cash-poor didn't you understand?'

'Yes, but I assumed your friends would have offered you opportunities—like on that trip to London, for instance. You hardly carried all your own shopping home on a commercial flight.'

Eva shot him a look across the table between them. It was explicit. *Not. Going. There.*

She was even less inclined to tell him the truth now. He'd laugh if he realised she'd had nothing as frivolous as shopping to bring home. And that she'd flown with a budget airline, squeezed into the middle of three seats.

It had been hard for her to focus since they'd left Vidal's London apartment and driven out of the city to the small airfield where this sleek jet had been waiting for them.

The insides were all cream leather. Carpet so

thick it was like walking on a cloud. Polished wood finishes. Discreet staff.

Vidal said, 'This calls for a celebration.' He pressed a button and a man in a uniform materialised as if from thin air.

'Sir? What can I get you?'

'Two glasses of champagne please, Tom.' Just as the man was turning to leave Vidal said, 'Actually, Tom, let me introduce you. This is Eva Flores. Eva—meet Tom.'

Eva's face felt hot, but she forced a smile. It wasn't the man's fault. Vidal was making a point. 'Very nice to meet you.'

'And you, Miss Flores. I'll be right back.'

Eva looked at Vidal and smiled sweetly. 'Thank you for that.'

For a moment he had an arrested expression on his face and her smile faded.

'What is it? What have I done now?'

He shook his head. And then he said, 'You don't smile very much. Do you know that?'

Eva's chest felt tight. She shrugged as if she didn't care. 'I'm sure I smile as much as the next person.' But she knew she didn't. Before she could stop herself she was saying, 'My mother told me that smiling would give me wrinkles.'

She'd also told her that smiling made her look gormless. She kept that to herself.

Tom returned with two glasses of honey-hued

champagne on a tray and handed her one. She took it and smiled again. It did feel a little…unnatural. She made a mental vow to herself to try and smile as much as possible from now on. To unnerve Vidal as much as anything else.

'Here's to a successful collaboration,' Vidal said.

Eva looked at him. 'I didn't know you were such a romantic.'

'Oh, I can be romantic when I want to be.'

The thought of Vidal caring about a woman enough to want to be romantic made Eva feel a little volatile. She took a sip of champagne. Then she put her glass down. She said, 'So how will it work for you? You don't even like me but you're happy to sleep with me?'

'Haven't you heard?' he asked with a mocking tone. 'Men don't need their emotions to be involved. Only their—'

Eva put up a hand. 'Yes, I get it.'

'Sex and emotions are two separate issues. But generally I sleep with women I like. I never said I didn't like you, Eva. What I feel about you is… complex. And challenging. But we don't need to worry about emotions in this instance. All we need is the chemistry that's been between us since the day we first met.'

Eva's breathing felt a little shallow. Had Vidal noticed it even then? Before she'd even been aware of what it was she was feeling? She'd only known it was somehow illicit.

'Don't you care what I might feel about you?' she asked.

Vidal shrugged. 'Not really. I don't need you to like me. I just need you to want me—which you do, but you won't admit it yet.'

I don't need you to like me.

Right at that moment Eva wasn't even sure what she *did* feel for Vidal. *Like* was such an ineffectual word for a feeling which was dark and complicated and intense. She couldn't even hope to articulate it.

'I won't sleep with you,' she said.

Because that would be far too exposing.

'I note you didn't say, *I don't want to sleep with you.* At least you're not lying to yourself about this.'

Eva flushed and avoided Vidal's eye.

'Maybe you'll fall in love with me, Eva, in spite of yourself.'

An electric shock went through her system at the thought of that. Of losing herself so completely. She speared him with a look. 'Fall in love with you? Why would you even want that?'

Vidal shrugged. 'It would amuse me, after all these years of you lodging yourself under my skin like a briar.'

Eva skittered away from such a ridiculous possibility. He was teasing her. 'You throw around the word "love" very easily,' she said.

'Love *is* easy.'

'How would you know?'

Eva had to admit that she was fascinated by this turn in the conversation.

'I saw love between my parents. They supported and respected each other and they were kind to each other. A small thing, but profound. How many couples do you see being kind to one another?'

Eva was speechless. All she could think of was the screaming match between her father and her mother before he'd walked out. He'd said so many awful things to her mother that day that Eva had blocked them out of her memory. She couldn't remember now even if she wanted to. They certainly hadn't been kind to each other. Or her.

'Not many,' she had to concede.

'I won't settle for anything less than the kind of love I witnessed between my parents. Even after she died, my father wasn't bitter. He celebrated her life and their love.'

Hearing Vidal admit such a thing so easily impacted on Eva somewhere very vulnerable.

'How old were you when she died?' she asked.

'Twelve.'

'I'm sorry.'

Now Vidal avoided her eye. 'It was a long time ago.'

'I won't fall in love with you, Vidal. What you describe… I saw the opposite. The lack of love. I don't believe it exists.'

Vidal took a sip of champagne. 'Don't underestimate yourself, Eva. You're only human.'

She rolled her eyes at that. 'What would you do even if I did? What if I became over-emotional and needy and didn't want to let you go?'

'I'm good at extricating myself from any relationship I don't want to be in any more.'

She didn't doubt it. She'd seen a whole new side to Vidal. He hadn't even tried to charm her and still she was doing his bidding, debating whether or not she'd sleep with him or, worse, fall in love.

You are getting something in return, reminded a voice.

Eva had almost forgotten what the objective was. She felt exposed and naive. She was already on a plane en route to America and Vidal had given her no assurances yet.

She sat up straight. 'What about the sale of the *castillo*? Have you been in touch with my solicitor?'

'It's all in hand. My solicitor in Spain is meeting with yours today. I'll have some contracts for you to sign when we get to San Francisco.'

Eva felt even more silly now. It was obvious she'd forgotten the objective here. To gain her freedom—economically and mentally. If that was possible.

'You don't trust me, Eva?'

She felt pinned under his mocking gaze. 'I would have without question before. But things are different now. *You're* different.'

'You're different too. At first I thought only superficially…but now I can see it.'

Eva didn't want to ask Vidal to elaborate, not sure she'd like his assessment. Not sure if it would be a positive or negative thing.

'There's a bedroom in the back if you want to get some rest. We'll be announcing our engagement at a very select press conference when we arrive at the airport. I figured it would be best to do it like that and get it out of the way—nip any speculation in the bud.'

Eva sat bolt upright. 'You're announcing it when we arrive? But what about…? I don't have anything with me except for that dress I wore last night…'

Vidal waved a hand. 'I had my assistant drop some clothes off in your size—you'll find them in the bedroom. Choose whatever you think is suitable.'

Eva felt panic rise. 'But that's just it. I don't

know what's suitable. I can't trust myself when it comes to fashion.'

'What are you talking about?'

'I had a bad experience when I was eighteen,' she divulged reluctantly. 'I turned up to a very exclusive party wearing the worst possible thing. Years out of date. I was ridiculed…'

It sounded so trite now, but at the time it had been traumatic enough to give her a complex.

'I just don't know if I have the best judgement.'

'Maybe you're right,' Vidal said thoughtfully.

Suddenly Eva felt defensive. 'What's that supposed to mean?'

'The dress you wore in London at the party with your father…that was pretty tacky.'

Eva bit her lip again. *That* dress hadn't been her fault. She'd known it was hideous. But she'd had no choice. If it could even have been called a dress. Two pieces of silver lamé held together with silver circlets that had run up and down each side of her body. Two thin straps were all that had held it up. It had been indecently short.

Then Vidal frowned. 'The dress you wore last night was perfectly acceptable.'

'That's because the girl in the hire-shop helped me to pick it out.'

To Eva's surprise, Vidal stood up and held out

a hand. She looked at it, scared of touching him when she felt so exposed.

'Come on,' he said, sounding perfectly reasonable.

Eva knew she was being ridiculous. That the more of a deal she made of it the more he'd know he affected her.

She slipped her hand into his and immediately regretted it. Little sparks of electricity raced up her arm and her lower body tensed. She let him pull her up. They were too close. She realised that she was so much smaller than him, even though she was relatively tall.

If she stepped right into his body her head would tuck in perfectly under his chin. She was overcome with a need to do that, and slide her arms around his waist...

But he was tugging her down the aisle, and she sent up silent thanks that he hadn't seen that moment of weakness. He opened the door and Eva gasped when a luxurious bedroom was revealed. Complete with a spacious en suite bathroom.

Vidal let her hand go. She pretended not to notice, even though it still tingled. 'Wow...this is...impressive.'

Vidal was standing by a rail of clothes. Eva approached with trepidation. She seriously thought she had some kind of dyslexia when it came to clothes and colours.

Vidal pulled out a royal blue trouser suit and held it up in front of Eva. He made a face and put it back. Then he pulled out a knee-length leather skirt and a cashmere top.

'That's nice,' Eva said, reaching out to touch the top.

But Vidal was already putting it back on the rail, muttering something about it being too much like a work outfit.

Then he pulled out a dress—it had short sleeves and was dressy without being too over the top. Lots of different colours.

Vidal handed it to her. 'Try this, with this...' he pulled out a short jacket '...and these...' He added a pair of high-heeled shoes in a colour matching the dress.

Eva held the clothes and shoes in her arms and Vidal made a rotating motion with his finger. 'Bathroom—behind you. I'll wait here.'

Eva went into the bathroom, bemused. It was only when she was standing in her underwear that she realised nothing but a thin piece of board and plastic and a few feet separated her from Vidal. And a massive bed.

She hurriedly pulled on the dress, but when she went to pull up the zip she couldn't reach it. Blowing a stray hair out of her eyes in exasperation, Eva put her hands on her hips.

'Do you need help?' Vidal called.

Eva grimaced. 'Yes.'

'Come out.'

The dress was modest from the front, covering her from the neck down, but it was short, coming to mid-thigh. And the skin of her exposed back prickled. But she couldn't hide in here for ever.

She opened the door. 'I can't do up the zip.'

'Turn around.'

Eva did as Vidal bade, and presented him with her back. For a long moment he did nothing, and then she felt his fingers come to the bottom of the zip, resting just above the small of her back.

She tried to repress a shiver of awareness as he slowly drew up the zip. She was very aware of her plain white bra strap. No doubt he was used to more exciting underwear. She wouldn't have a clue where to start buying anything sexy. Not that she wanted to.

Vidal pulled the zip all the way to the top of her back and pushed her hair over one shoulder. His fingers lingered at the nape of her neck for a moment. Eva stopped breathing. But then his hands fell away and she sensed him moving back.

'Turn around.'

She did. The dress was not like anything she'd have chosen for herself. It clung to every dip and hollow. Vidal's gaze was slowly travelling down over her belly and thighs. And back up.

'You look perfect,' he said.

'Is it appropriate?'

He said, 'With the jacket, it'll be fine.'

The air between them felt thick and charged. The space that had at first seemed cavernous suddenly felt tiny. The bed loomed large in Eva's peripheral vision.

Then he said, 'I have something else that you'll need.'

He turned around and took a box from the top of a cabinet. A small box with the distinctively familiar colours and logo of one of the world's most famous and iconic jewellers. Devilliers.

Eva looked down when Vidal opened the box. She couldn't stop her mouth opening. It was a ring with a glittering yellow stone, square-shaped and set in gold, with white diamonds on either side.

'What stone is that?'

Eva was trying not to let Vidal see how confusing this was for her. She'd never dreamt of a moment like this, but suddenly she was realising that somewhere in the deepest recesses of her imagination she *had* allowed herself to imagine such a scenario. She'd dared to dream that some day someone might want her enough to propose. Give her a ring. Not because it was an arranged marriage but because they loved her.

She burned with mortification to acknowledge that futile dream now. To acknowledge that she'd been that weak. Even though her mother had told her over and over again that love didn't exist. Not for people like them.

Vidal believed in love. Believed he would find it. That it was his due.

That only sent Eva's emotions into a deeper spiral.

'It's a yellow diamond.'

Vidal's voice cut through the rising panic inside Eva. She took a deep breath. 'It's beautiful.'

Vidal took it out of the box and held it up. Suddenly Eva's dream felt very real, but very fake all at once.

She reached for the ring. 'You don't have to. I can put it on.'

'I want to.'

Eva glared at Vidal, but finally gave him her hand. It felt very small and delicate in his. She was conscious of her short, functional nails. It felt like a travesty putting such a beautiful ring on such a hand, but the ring slid on and fitted perfectly. Like in a fairy tale. But this was no fairy tale. This was a parody. A punishment. A retribution.

She tried to pull her hand back. He wouldn't let go. She looked at him. He was very close. His eyes were on her mouth and it tingled.

His gaze moved up. 'You know, there's something I owe you.'

Eva's head felt fuzzy. She couldn't think straight. 'You don't owe me anything.'

He nodded and moved closer. 'I do, actually.'

Eva's breath stopped.

'I owe you a kiss.'

Eva tried to move her head, to shake it. 'It's okay, you really don't.'

'But you were so angry that day when I wouldn't kiss you back.'

'I misread the situation.'

'You didn't misread anything. You just caught me by surprise. Do you want to know why I didn't kiss you back?'

'I… Okay…' Eva's tongue felt heavy. She couldn't stop her gaze from moving down to Vidal's mouth. Sculpted and firm. Full.

'Because I wanted to…too much. And you weren't ready. You'd pushed me to the edges of my control. And that day… I almost lost it,' he said. 'But now you're ready.'

Am I? Eva wondered through the haze in her head.

Vidal was moving even closer and sliding a hand under her hair, cupping her jaw, moving a thumb back and forth along her skin. His other hand was on her waist. She was in her bare feet, and he tipped her chin up just before his head lowered towards hers, and Eva was drowning in his eyes, blue and green.

She'd pressed her mouth to his all those years ago and it had been so shockingly inflammatory that she could still recall the burst of heat in her lower body. But it had ended almost as soon as it had begun, when Vidal had pulled back.

You weren't ready...but now you're ready.

His mouth hovered a heart-stopping inch above Eva's. Her head was tipped back, her body curving towards his. Every cell clamoured for his touch. She craved to know what it would feel like to kiss him. She'd dreamed of this even as she'd burned with humiliation because of his rejection.

She'd seen it as a slight—a petty way to pay her back for all of the ways she'd reminded him of his place. But in hindsight he'd never been petty. He'd been confident. He'd pulled back because she hadn't been ready for him. For what he'd wanted to do.

That thought was dizzying and Eva almost fell. But at the last second she remembered that the only thing she had to cling on to was her dignity. If she gave in to Vidal now he would have won. She would be lost.

Abruptly, still dizzy with need, Eva pulled back, dislodging Vidal's hands. The air crackled around them, thick with electricity. She almost felt that if she touched something solid she'd get a shock, it was that tangible.

Vidal didn't seem to be concerned. He stood back. Watching. She felt undone. How on earth would she react if he actually touched her? The prospect was as terrifying as it was exhilarating.

'I told you, I won't sleep with you.'

Supremely confident, Vidal said, 'You will. Of that I have no doubt.' His gaze swept her up and down. 'That dress is perfect by the way. You might just want to fix your hair.'

He was gone and the door had closed behind him before Eva could take another breath. In a fit of irritation at Vidal's sanguinity, and frustration at the way her body ached for fulfilment, Eva picked up a sandal and launched it at the door.

It fell to the ground ineffectually and Eva heard a low chuckle from the other side of the door.

She clenched her hands and went into the bathroom. She groaned. They hadn't even kissed and her hair looked as if she'd been tumbled backwards through a bush. Her cheeks were pink and her eyes were overbright.

She could never claim that she didn't want Vidal—they both knew that she did—but by God she would die before giving in to it. Because she knew deep in her bones that once that happened she would be risking the destruction of every emotional wall that had kept her intact her whole life.

And she certainly wasn't ready for that.

Vidal went back and sat in his seat, his body filled with pumping blood and frustration. She was playing him. She had to be. She wasn't an ardent teenager any more. She was a woman. And something about that stuck in Vidal's gut like a splinter.

What? he asked himself. Did he regret not being the one to initiate her when she'd all but thrown herself at him?

No, he assured himself. Because he knew exactly how it would have gone. She would have stood up afterwards, made some cutting remark and walked away, having absorbed the experience the way she did everything—as if it was her due.

Hell, she'd probably assumed at the time that it was Vidal's duty to initiate her, so that she would be free to get on with seducing an appropriate husband. Except that didn't appear to have happened.

She and her mother had gone into a decline before Eva could establish herself. Did he feel sorry for her? No. What she'd gone through was no more or less than most mortals. And she'd still had a roof over head. She still had her name and her lineage, like a talisman.

A lineage you're only too happy to take advantage of, mocked an inner voice.

Vidal picked up the champagne and took a large gulp. It tasted bitter when paired with sexual frustration.

Yet she hadn't appeared bitter about working in the hotel. She'd seemed…resigned to it. So maybe her experience had smoothed a few edges. Given her a much-needed perspective on the world and the privilege she'd taken for granted.

The door to the bedroom opened and Vidal looked up. Eva emerged in the dress and jacket and shoes, looking immaculate. Legs impossibly long and shapely. Hair slicked back and tucked behind her ears. Expression as smooth as silk. Every inch the regal scion of an illustrious bloodline.

She stood by the table and gestured to herself, 'This will do?'

Vidal consciously didn't let his gaze drop, even though it took physical effort. The colours of the dress made her eyes look even more golden. She was breathtakingly stunning.

'That'll do.'

She said, 'Thank you for arranging the clothes.'

So polite. For a second, disconcertingly, Vidal was reminded of what she'd been like as a young teenager. Immaculately polite but with a tongue as sharp as a razor. He was almost waiting for her to say something else, but she didn't.

'You're welcome. It's the least I can do to ensure you feel comfortable in public.'

She went slightly pale at that, but before he could question it Eva said, 'If that's all for now, I think I'll lie down until it's time to land.'

'Be my guest.'

She turned and went back down the aisle of the plane and disappeared into the bedroom, leaving Vidal curiously deflated. Sometimes she was as easy to read as a book, and then, like a picture jarring out of focus for a second, it was as if she was someone else. Any hint of revealing anything a mere illusion.

But she could keep her illusions. He didn't care what was going on—he only cared that she fulfilled her part of their mutually beneficial arrangement and, when the time came, surrendered to him and sated the fire in his blood.

He chose not to acknowledge his sense of anticipation of that final moment of capitulation, telling himself it was ridiculous to think that it would eclipse everything he'd experienced up to now, personally or professionally.

Eva was still in shock at the sheer number of press waiting for them at the airport in San Francisco. They'd landed a short time before and some of Vidal's staff had come onto the plane to brief them—all very officious and efficient.

The press were waiting in a huddle at the bottom of the steps to the plane. It was meant to be informal. But Eva didn't feel informal. Her palms were clammy with nerves.

She hadn't slept much in spite of her attempts. Too wound up after that almost-kiss with Vidal. His control had mocked hers. Did he really want her at all, or was he just enjoying watching her tie herself in knots?

She put on the jacket over the dress and saw that Vidal was holding out his hand. 'Ready?'

The engagement ring felt heavy on her finger. She knew they were meant to be presenting a united front, so she couldn't very well avoid touching Vidal. She put her hand in his and tensed against the inevitable *zing* of awareness.

He led her to the door of the plane and the world exploded into flashes of light. Eva flinched. The only time she'd been photographed in a similar way had been in London on that ill-fated trip to see her father.

Not the time to think of that.

Vidal led her down the steps of the plane to the bottom. A PR person directed the questions and Vidal answered smoothly. They'd decided to keep things as true as possible, saying that they'd met when he and his father had lived at the *castillo*.

Vidal said now, 'It was a long friendship that has just recently blossomed into something much deeper. I'm honoured that Eva has agreed to be my wife.'

'When are you getting married?'

Eva felt Vidal tense beside her. But he said smoothly, 'There's plenty of time to make plans...we're going to enjoy our engagement.'

Eva was surprised to find that she was almost believing Vidal. He sounded so...authentic. For a second she was imagining... What if they really had been friends? What if she'd been allowed to talk to him as she'd wanted to on many occasions? Was this some kind of parallel fantasy existence?

And then he turned to her. He said something she didn't catch and then he was cupping her chin, tipping it up.

He arched a brow. 'Ready?'

There was a look on his face that was somewhere between tender and hungry. It disarmed Eva completely.

She wanted to resist...she knew it was important to resist...but it was too late. Vidal's firm, warm mouth was settling over hers and Eva's brain ceased functioning. He didn't deepen the kiss, just held it there for a long moment. And then pulled back.

It took a second for Eva to open her eyes, and when she did she was almost blinded by the pops of light. Vidal's PR person was stepping in and saying something about that being all for now... giving the couple their privacy...and Vidal was leading her over to an SUV with tinted windows.

A driver in a suit was holding open the back door and Vidal helped her in, before closing the door and going around to the other side. Then they were moving smoothly out of the airport and towards the tall buildings Eva could see in the distance.

'Are you okay?' he asked.

Eva felt a bit dazed. Vidal took her hand. She looked at him. 'I'm not used to that.'

'No... I guess not. Sorry, I probably should have prepared you better.'

Eva shook her head. 'It's fine.'

She pulled her hand back, liking how it felt in his too much. She'd learnt a long time ago not to seek comfort or reassurance because her mother had never given it. Another weakness.

She could still feel the impression of Vidal's mouth on hers. Like a brand. It had precipitated a longing such as she'd never felt before. It went deeper than desire. And that was scary.

It was early evening in San Francisco and the

sky was a blaze of colour. Eva let herself be distracted as they drove into the city, through the iconic Haight-Ashbury hippy area and the famously vertiginous streets.

Soon they were in a surprisingly quiet, residential part of the city and the car came to a stop outside a very discreet fence with high trees. The gate opened and a man in dark trousers and a matching polo shirt came out.

Vidal greeted him warmly and then came around to help Eva out of the car. He introduced her to the man. 'This is Michael, my house manager.'

The man inclined his head and smiled. 'Miss Flores, it's a pleasure to welcome you here, and congratulations on your engagement.'

Eva shook the man's hand, embarrassed. Surely he must know this was a total sham? They'd never even met before!

He went back in through the gate, carrying their luggage, and Vidal led the way into a space that made Eva's jaw drop. Behind the high fence and the trees was a modern work of art set amidst immaculately landscaped gardens. Stone and glass and steel. Huge front doors.

Eva followed Vidal, entranced, as he led her into a massive double-height foyer. It was modern and minimalist without feeling cold or as if one shouldn't touch anything. The furnishings were tactile and comfortable-looking. Art decorated the walls that weren't glass. And as he led her through the ground floor to the other side of the house they came out to the back, where there was a balcony. Looking down, Eva could see a lower level with a long lap pool.

Silent, she could feel Vidal watching her reaction. Then he said, 'You probably hate it.'

Eva shook her head. 'No, I…really like it.'

'Let me show you upstairs.'

Without thinking, Eva slipped off her high-heeled sandals and followed Vidal in bare feet. He looked back at her and clearly noted the feet. She felt self-conscious. 'Do you mind? The shoes were pinching and I don't want to ruin your floors.'

He shook his head, looking a little bemused. 'Not at all. This is your home too…for the next few weeks.'

Few weeks. Maybe Vidal was already regretting his impetuous plan to fake an engagement with her. Maybe he was already deciding that a week or two would be enough.

They went up to the next level, where there was a comfortable lounge area with a massive TV and media system. And then up another level. Vidal walked her through a formal dining area to a decked area outside. The air was still balmy, even though autumn was closing in.

There was outdoor seating and a fire pit, but Eva went straight over to the glass railing and took in the view of the Golden Gate Bridge in the near distance, and all the grid-like streets and houses in between.

Eva said, 'I can see why they called this the New World. It *feels* like a new world.'

And it did. She felt as if a weight had been lifted off her shoulders. A crazy sensation for a property to bestow. But it was true. It couldn't be more opposite to the *castillo*—and maybe that was why it appealed to her so much.

'You surprise me.'

Eva looked at Vidal, who was watching her. 'Why?' she asked. 'Because you assumed I'd only feel at home in buildings that date back hundreds of years?' She shuddered lightly. 'No. Give me the new any day.'

There was a sound behind them, and Eva turned around to see Michael approach.

'Sorry to intrude, boss, but your car is waiting.'

Vidal emitted a soft curse and looked at his watch, then back to Eva. 'I'm afraid I have to go to a meeting with my board, but Michael will show you your room and prepare something to eat. I'll see you in the morning.'

And then he was walking away through the vast open-plan space, leaving Eva feeling adrift.

Michael smiled and said, 'Please, let me show you to your room and then we can discuss your dietary requirements.'

She forced a smile and followed Michael, trying not to let echoes of the past reverberate through her head, when she'd invariably been left to her own devices.

Vidal was not her mother, this was not the *castillo*, and she was not a child any more. She could handle this.

CHAPTER SIX

THE FOLLOWING MORNING, Vidal still couldn't shake the niggling of his conscience at the way he'd left Eva so abruptly last night. She'd looked surprised. A little lost. And he'd almost forgotten he had a meeting, because he'd been so transfixed by watching her reaction to his house.

He'd expected her to be blasé. Judgemental. But she'd seemed enchanted. In fact... He had to concede that the Eva Flores he'd met over a week ago was proving to be quite the enigma.

One minute he thought she was the same cold and aloof girl he'd known, ready to reel him in only to lash out with a sting in the tail, and the next she seemed like someone who bore no resemblance to that person. Someone entirely new.

It was disconcerting.

He heard a sound and looked up from where he sat at the breakfast table, near the lap pool on the bottom terrace. Eva was walking towards him wearing faded jeans and a plain white shirt. Hair down, silky. Simple, classic.

Her face was expressionless and old instincts kicked in. The urge to protect himself while at the same time wanting to get underneath that smooth facade. He'd never met anyone who did it so well as her. She could give a masterclass in superiority without even saying a word. Her mother had been the same.

And he'd almost been feeling sorry for her!

She sat in a chair.

'Good morning,' he said, as his chef came to the table with some freshly baked pastries.

'Santo, this is Eva.'

Eva looked up at Santo and smiled. 'Nice to meet you, Santo.'

Vidal saw the man do a double take at Eva's stunning smile. He almost did a double take himself. Santo left and Vidal caught Eva's eye.

Her smile faded. 'What?'

He shook his head. 'Nothing.' And then, 'Did you sleep well?'

Her eyes widened. He noticed she wore no make-up. She was so naturally beautiful that she really was breathtaking.

'My rooms are…amazing. I'm not used to such modern comforts.'

Vidal realised that the *castillo* might be impressive—but no one could describe it as comfortable. 'I guess not. But you don't ever have to go back to that lifestyle. Speaking of which, my legal team have the contracts detailing the terms of our agreement at my office. Your solicitor has sent an envoy from a firm here to represent you and make sure you're happy with everything. We'll go to the office after this.'

'Okay…'

She sounded hesitant. 'You're not changing your mind?' Vidal asked.

She shook her head and took a sip of coffee. 'No, I just…can't believe that it's all happening so quickly and easily. The debts are…big.' She looked at him. 'Are you sure *you're* not changing your mind? After all, I don't know that my presence by your side is really going to be worth all that much.'

Vidal told himself that her self-deprecation was just a smokescreen. That maybe she was looking for something more.

He shook his head. 'Not at all. It's a viable business venture, I'm fulfilling my father's wishes, and I will have you on my arm to demonstrate how socially acceptable I am in order to secure an important investment. A win for both of us.'

Silently he added, *And I will have you in my bed, to burn this permanent ache from my body and cool the fire in my blood.*

But it was as if his thoughts had silently communicated themselves to Eva. Her cheeks went pink and she said, 'That's it? By your side? Not in your bed?'

Anticipation sizzled along Vidal's veins. 'Like I said, I have never forced a woman into my bed. They've all come quite willingly. And with great enthusiasm.'

It took her a second to absorb his double meaning and her cheeks went even pinker. 'That's disgusting!'

Vidal was intrigued by her prudishness. 'Not disgusting at all. I like to ensure that my lovers are very well—'

The sound of Santo returning with fresh coffee cut Vidal off. He almost laughed out loud at the murderous look in Eva's eyes. It was going to be *so* satisfying when she capitulated and begged him to make love to her.

When Santo was gone again, Vidal leaned forward and said, 'Don't forget that I've seen all that fire and passion inside you, Eva Flores. You might be able to fool others with that scandalised innocent act, but you can't fool me.'

Eva's hand stopped in the process of moving to her mouth with a pastry. She went very still inside. 'You mean…when I tried to kiss you…?'

But Vidal shook his head.

Genuinely confused, Eva started to say, 'But what—?' And then she broke off. Because she had thought of something.

But surely there was no way that Vidal... The thought of him knowing about that made her feel sick. And more exposed than she'd ever felt in her life. It was her deepest secret. Deeper even than the hopes and dreams she'd told herself she didn't harbour.

She looked at him and shook her head, but he nodded. There was a gleam in his eye. He said, 'I used to watch you.'

Eva kept on shaking her head, thinking of how in those moments she'd felt so elemental. Free. Once Vidal's father had stumbled across her secret place, and she'd got such a fright that—to her shame—she'd threatened to have him fired if he ever told anyone.

She tried to bluff. 'I don't know what you're talking about.'

'Do you still do it?'

No. She didn't. But she dreamt of it often. That feeling of losing herself in the beat and music.

She tried again. 'I don't know what you're talking about.'

'Who first taught you to dance like that, Eva? I know you were teaching yourself when I used to watch you, because you were using online tutorials. You were so determined... I've never seen you look so intent about anything. But someone must have taught you first.'

Eva wanted to curl in on herself and protect that very secret part of her—the part that had loved doing something so forbidden.

But, very reluctantly, she divulged, 'It was our first housekeeper. Maria. She was gone by the time you arrived. I saw her one day, dancing in the kitchen. And she used to sing. Such sad songs... I asked her to show me what she was doing.'

'How old were you?'

'About eight.'

It had been shortly after her father had left and her mother had taken to her bedroom, where there had been either long silences or ranting and raving. Maria had been the only one who had cared for Eva through that time. Until one day when Eva had been down in the kitchen with Maria, who was showing her how to cook something, and her mother had appeared and said coldly, 'The kitchen is not a suitable environment for my daughter. And *I* am her mother. Maria, you may go.'

Eva had been inconsolable. Her mother had slapped her across the face to stop her crying and Eva had never cried again. She'd bottled up all her emotions deep inside and made sure she never showed anything that would enrage her mother.

'You were very good, you know,' said Vidal.

'I… Thank you. No one knew. I didn't want anyone to know.'

'Why?'

Eva emitted a short sharp laugh. 'Can you imagine my mother if she'd seen that? Her daughter? Dancing Flamenco? She would have cast me out of the *castillo* on the spot. Like she did Maria.'

Vidal frowned. 'She fired Maria?'

Eva nodded. 'She didn't like her influence on me.'

'You were a *child*.'

'I was ten when she fired Maria, and those couple of years when she was with us were probably the happiest I can remember in that place.'

Until Vidal had arrived with his father, and Eva had felt as if she was coming out of a fog. The world had suddenly looked sharper again. And that was when she'd started practising Flamenco again on her own. As if to try and understand or channel all the things she was feeling.

But she didn't mention that. The fact that he'd seen her in those moments was shocking. But also… She'd fantasised when she'd been dancing that he was watching her. Maybe on some subliminal level she'd known? And had revelled in it?

Suddenly it was too much. It was as if Vidal had prised her open and taken out her most precious secret to inspect under fluorescent lighting.

Her voice clipped, she said, 'I don't do it any more.'

'That's a pity. Maybe you'll dance for me sometime.'

She looked at him, her insides clenching at the thought. 'Never.'

'So if you'll just sign here, Miss Flores...'

The solicitor handed her a pen and Eva hesitated only for the barest moment before signing away the property that had been in her mother's family for generations. She felt nothing. Not an ounce of guilt or sentimentality. Just a little numb.

The agreement was more than generous, considering the fact that Vidal didn't owe her a thing. The debts were cleared and she was being given an option of taking a stake in the new business once it was up and running, and a position on the board of managers if she wanted.

Right now, she felt as if she never wanted anything to do with the *castillo* again, but she was wise enough not to burn her bridges.

She was finally free. For the first time in her

life. But that numb feeling persisted…as if it was too huge to absorb.

There was a knock on the door and she and her solicitor looked up to see Vidal enter.

The solicitor stood up and closed the folder holding all the documents. 'I think that's everything. I'll check with Miss Flores's representative in Madrid and let you know if there are any loose ends.'

'Thank you.' Vidal closed the door behind the middle-aged man.

The numb feeling started to dissipate as Eva took Vidal in. He was wearing a suit and they had come to his offices, located in the buzzing Mission district. Eva wasn't surprised that Vidal had chosen to be in the hub of the city rather than out in the suburbs where most of the tech companies were based.

'Thank you,' Eva said, beginning to feel the magnitude of what had just happened sinking in.

'You don't mind that you've just signed away hundreds of years of legacy?'

Eva stood up and went over to a window that looked out on a green courtyard area in the middle of the complex. Staff were sitting on the grass eating their lunch. Carefree. Now she could be like them. Except she had to navigate the small matter of resisting Vidal Suarez for a few weeks first.

She turned around. 'Truthfully? No. I'm sorry I can't pretend otherwise. It was not a happy place. Your father obviously saw a vision of how it could have been…and if you can bring it back to some kind of life and benefit people then that'll be good.'

Vidal rested his hips against the desk and folded his arms. 'You always looked very content in your role as lady of the manor in waiting. But you're saying you weren't happy?'

What a loaded question. Eva wasn't even sure how to answer. 'I didn't know anything else. The *castillo* was my world. I wasn't aware of being happy or unhappy.'

But that wasn't entirely true. She knew she'd been happy whenever she'd seen Vidal arrive back at the *castillo* during his holidays.

That had been her first real awareness of the two states—happiness and unhappiness. And she'd been happy when she'd danced. Or when she'd been in the kitchen with Maria, learning how to cook. And dance.

With her mother, she'd never felt any happiness. She'd felt tense. On guard. Pressure in her chest. Wary.

Feeling the past sucking her under, Eva said, 'So what happens now?'

Vidal stood up. 'I have a pretty packed social schedule for the next week—so you're going shopping.'

Immediately Eva felt a sense of panic. 'Vidal, I'm really not—'

'I've enlisted a stylist to go with you.'

'Oh.' Eva knew she should feel mildly insulted, or even ashamed that she didn't have the confidence to know what to buy or wear, but she was too relieved.

'How will I know—?'

'She has a list of the events we're attending and she knows the scene. It'll be fine. I'll meet you for lunch.'

Eva couldn't stop a little burst of surprise. And pleasure. 'I'm sure you're busy…you don't have to.'

'It's fine. I've booked a suitably visible place—it'll be good for us to be seen together as much as possible.'

'Oh, of course.' The burst of pleasure fizzled away.

'So why are you so paranoid about what to wear in public?'

Eva was very conscious of the scrutiny that she and Vidal were under at a table in prime position on the terrace of a very exclusive restaurant on the waterfront. The paparazzi across the street weren't even attempting to hide.

'Um…because of scenarios exactly like this!' Eva said, rolling her eyes.

Vidal raised a brow, obviously waiting for her to go on. Up to now, Eva had to admit that they'd passed quite a pleasant time, conversing about general topics. The stylist was meeting her again after lunch, to continue shopping, and for this lunch date she'd changed into flared trousers and a loose-fitting silky top. Surprisingly comfortable.

'I told you—there was an event when I was eighteen. I thought my dress was perfectly nice. My mother approved. It was only when I got there that I realised how out of touch I was with…*everything*. I hadn't really been out in society since before I was a teenager.'

'You were being home-schooled and you had no friends.'

Eva looked at Vidal. He knew too much. 'Thank you for that reminder.'

He shrugged, as if he hadn't just spoken one of her biggest vulnerabilities out loud. He said, 'I used to feel sorry for you, but then you'd invariably say something cutting and make me remember that you didn't need pity from anyone.'

No—because she'd become adept at maintaining that prickly barrier at all costs. In case Vidal got too close. In case her mother decided he should be humiliated again, like at that dinner.

Eva's conscience hurt as it always did when she thought of that night. She couldn't help saying, 'That dinner that my mother invited you to…before you went back to university…'

'Yes?'

Eva forced herself to look at him. 'I've always wanted to apologise for that evening. I had no idea she was going to use it to just…ignore you like that. To talk about you as if you weren't even there. It was…not nice.'

'I remember you sitting there, avoiding my eye. Why didn't you say something?'

'I was sixteen.'

Vidal was quiet, and then he said, 'You know, I always felt you were older in so many ways. And then at the same time younger. A contradiction.'

She'd felt very young that night. Out of her depth. Hating what her mother was doing but not knowing how to stop it. Wearing a dress that she'd been excited to wear in front of Vidal but realising as soon as he'd walked in that it was all wrong. Too fussy. Too formal. Too young. She'd wanted to be sexy.

Maybe that had been the start of her complex about knowing what to wear?

Vidal popped a grape into his mouth. 'So you're saying that you and your mother weren't co-conspirators, then?'

'Truthfully, how I feel about my mother is complicated. She was all I knew. I trusted her. She told me how to be.'

'My father used to tell me that it wasn't your fault. How could you know any different? And I would give you the benefit of the doubt, over and over again, only to be shut down.'

Eva squirmed. 'I don't think I knew what I was doing. I didn't know how to be any other way.'

Vidal leant forward. 'I think you *did* know what you were doing. At some point you made a decision that teasing me and torturing me and looking down your nose at me was more fun than actually attempting to be a nice person.'

Eva felt as if Vidal had slid a knife between her ribs. In many ways she could see it from his perspective, but she'd just told him more about how she felt about her complex past than she'd ever revealed to anyone else. And he clearly didn't want to revise his opinion.

As far as he knew, she had behaved as she had out of pure spite and badness. Not because she'd been coerced by her bitter mother and because she truly had not known she could be brave enough to trust her own instincts.

Eva had revealed far too much. Vidal was chipping away at her with his questions. And he didn't really care at all. She was just a means to an end. And he was a means to an end for her too. She needed to remember that.

She schooled her expression into one as close to boredom as she could get and looked at her phone. 'It's time for me to meet the stylist again. I should go.'

But before she could get up, Vidal reached across the table and entwined his fingers with hers, sending an electric shock straight between her legs.

'Wha—?'

Before she could even utter the word, Vidal had cupped her jaw with his other hand and was settling his mouth over hers, taking advantage of her surprise to make the kiss intimate. This was no peck on the lips. This was open and explicit and she had no defence.

The touch of his tongue to hers was fleeting, but devastating. Then he pulled back. It had lasted mere seconds—if even that long. Eva felt dizzy. Vidal smiled, but it was more like a smirk.

He kept hold of her hand as he stood up, tugging her up too.

A waiter materialised. 'The bill, Mr Suarez?'

Vidal didn't take his eyes off her, for all the world the besotted fiancé. 'Please… My fiancée here has a busy afternoon. I'm sorry we can't stay for dessert.'

'That is no problem at all, sir.'

Vidal led Eva out of the restaurant, and the heads of the other diners swivelled after them as they went.

Eva was too shell-shocked to do anything but follow in his wake. But when they got outside she recovered her wits. She pulled her hand out of his and said, 'That was sneaky.'

'It was an opportunity to make our union look authentic, and I took it.'

'Please do not do that again without asking me first. I don't like to be manhandled.'

A ghost of a smile made Vidal's mouth twitch. 'You didn't mind at the time.'

Heat pulsed between Eva's legs. No, she hadn't minded at all. That was the problem.

'Haven't you heard? There's a little thing called consent now.'

Vidal stepped close and said, 'Fine. May I take your hand?'

Eva put it behind her back. 'Why?'

'Because there are photographers across the road with their lenses trained on us right now.'

She hesitated. 'What are you going to do with my hand?'

'With your consent, I'm going to lift it up and kiss your inner palm.'

Eva knew that they needed to be seen to be behaving like a real affianced couple. Otherwise what was the point?

She offered him her hand. 'Okay. But no kissing on the mouth again.'

Vidal lifted her hand to his mouth and turned her palm towards him, saying in a low voice, 'There are plenty of other places to kiss, besides on the mouth. It won't be a problem.'

And then she felt the warmth of his breath against her skin and he pressed his lips to her palm, lingering for a long moment. She felt the tip of his tongue and gasped. 'That's cheating.'

He let her go. 'See you back at the house later.'

Eva was still cursing Vidal that evening, while she waited for him in the lounge area. All afternoon she'd been tortured with a slew of X-rated images of him kissing various parts of her body.

When the stylist had taken her to a lingerie boutique it had got even worse. The stylist had ignored her protestations that she didn't need sexy underwear, and as she couldn't reveal why, she'd had to give in and let her do her thing.

Eva had found herself sighing over the wispiest bits of lace with ribbon ties, and bras that looked like works of art more than a device to support body parts. She'd never seen anything so decadent and beautiful.

Feeling guilty, because she'd known it would never be seen by anyone other than her, she'd allowed the stylist to box it all up and add it to the growing collection of boxes and bags.

She knew she was focusing on her irritation with Vidal to try and disguise her extreme anxiety at the thought of appearing in public with him at an event tonight. A charity ball, apparently, and one of San Francisco's glitziest annual social fixtures. And she was also trying to hide the lingering hurt of his opinion of her. But in a way she realised that she could use it to her advantage—as a buffer to keep him from getting any closer.

She heard a sound and turned around, and every rational thought in her head disappeared. Vidal was standing a few feet away in a classic black tuxedo. His full metamorphosis from the son of a humble grounds manager to a titan of industry was complete.

His suit had to be bespoke, because there was no point where the material didn't mould lovingly to his body and his muscles. He was... magnificent. Breathtaking.

His gaze was raking her up and down. Immediately Eva felt conscious, even though the stylist had come back with a hair and make-up team to help her get ready for this evening.

His eyes met hers. They stood out even more against the backdrop of black and white. He said, 'You look stunning, Eva. Truly.'

'I… Thank you.'

She'd been afraid the dress was too dramatic. Red and strapless, with a tight bodice, falling to the floor in a swathe of tulle over silk.

Eva had said to the stylist, 'I'd like to stay under the radar if I can.'

The woman had laughed, 'Standing beside Vidal Suarez? You haven't a hope. Not many could pull this dress off, but with your colouring it'll look spectacular.'

They'd left her hair down, artfully tousled. Thankfully, there was a minimum of make-up.

Vidal said, 'We should go—my driver is waiting.'

Emotion was rising in Eva's chest before she could stop it, and she realised it was a feeling of pride in Vidal that he would not thank her for.

Controlling her emotions had become much harder since her mother had died. It was as if suddenly Eva didn't have to hold on so tightly. As if a too-tight button had finally been released.

And seeing Vidal again was having an even more adverse effect on her being able to control…anything.

'*So* sorry for your loss. Your mother was the most beautiful debutante of her year… I remember it well.'

When the older woman had moved away, Eva said to Vidal, 'I have no idea who that person was.'

'But she knows who you are, which is the important thing.'

And it confirmed for Vidal that he was doing the right thing. *This* was why he had Eva by his side.

After lunch today he'd spent the afternoon distracted and doubting his instincts—*again*. He hadn't expected her to mention that humiliating dinner her mother had invited him to, or to express any remorse. It had been so demeaning, to sit there and listen to her talking about him as if he was invisible. So much so that even now, if he was at a dinner party, he always had a moment of insecurity...a feeling that he wasn't meant to be there. That people might just ignore him or talk over him.

Eva had always pushed his buttons, and there had been too many moments when he'd shown a moment's weakness towards her and she'd punished him for it for him to begin to review the past with different eyes. But there had been something vulnerable about her today, and the notion had lodged itself under his skin that perhaps things weren't as black and white as he'd like to think.

Irritated by the questions she'd thrown up, and by the way her face had become a bland mask again at the end of their lunch, his impulse to kiss her had been as much about that as an opportunity to solidify their fake engagement.

Now Eva's arm was through Vidal's as they moved through the crowd. She was holding on tight. Too tight. He looked down and could see the pinched lines of her face. She was tense. *No.* More than tense. She was scared.

I haven't really been out much in society.

Again, not the impression he'd had of her over these past years.

Not liking how his conscience was pricking at him, Vidal said irritably, 'You *can* smile, you know.'

Eva looked up at Vidal, surprised. 'I'm not smiling?'

'You rarely smile.'

'Maybe you should have chosen another woman to be your convenient fiancée, rather than someone who has a resting serious face.'

There she was. The Eva he knew.

You mean, the Eva you want to know...? suggested a snide voice.

Vidal ignored it. He stopped. 'Self-pity really doesn't suit you, Eva. And you're the only woman I want.'

Her cheeks turned pink. Immensely satisfying. Even when she said through gritted teeth, 'Not going to happen, Vidal.'

He shook his head. 'You really shouldn't back yourself into a corner—it'll make it so much more satisfying for me when you admit defeat.'

When they got back to the house later that evening, Vidal took some calls in his office. As he was going to bed he passed Eva's rooms and saw the door was partway open.

He found himself stopping, even though he hadn't intended to. He could see through to Eva's bathroom, where the door was open, and saw that she was reflected in the mirror. He could see her head and shoulders and face. She was wearing a silk night slip.

It took him a moment to realise that she was making faces at herself in the mirror. *No.* Not faces. She was smiling at herself. Or trying to. But the smiles looked forced and fake.

Then she emitted a sound of frustration, stuck her tongue out at herself and turned out the light.

Vidal quickly pulled the bedroom door closed, feeling as if he'd intruded on something very private.

A weight lodged in his gut that night, and as much as he tried to dismiss it, it wouldn't budge.

CHAPTER SEVEN

THE REST OF the week took on a routine as Eva settled into her new existence. An existence that she found to be far less oppressive than anything she'd expected or experienced before.

She loved the wide open skies of California and the irrepressibly friendly nature of almost everyone she met. She'd taken to walking around the neighbourhood during the day, when Vidal was either in his office in the house or at his offices downtown. When the first person had greeted her with an effusive *'Good morning!'* she hadn't known how to respond. She wasn't used to people addressing her so easily or so casually.

There was a green park near Vidal's house, and Eva had got into a routine of getting herself a latte from the local coffee shop and then sitting in the park while she drank it, watching the world go by. Having been sequestered in the *castillo* for most of her life, she found it fascinating.

She watched the mums, or—probably more likely in this area—the nannies with their children at the playground, their joyful shrieks piercing the air. One small, adorable boy had his two fathers with him.

Eva couldn't recall ever going to a playground as a child. She thought of Vidal's assessment… *self-pity doesn't suit you*…and scowled at herself.

Her childhood hadn't been conventional. She had her privilege to thank for that. But as she watched the children with their carers this morning, she couldn't help but feel an ache at the thought of all that she'd missed out on. Simple things—like going to a park.

A big shaggy collie-type dog ambled over and Eva smiled, reaching down to give it a scratch. He nudged against her, looking for more attention, and a woman rushed over.

'Ollie, leave that lady alone.' She grabbed the dog by the collar and started pulling him away.

Eva said, 'I don't mind, really.'

But the woman and the dog were gone.

'I didn't know you liked dogs.'

Eva nearly dropped her coffee. She looked up to see Vidal standing beside the bench, a cup of coffee in his own hand. She said, almost accusingly, 'I thought you were working.'

'I was. And then I went looking for you and Santo said you'd gone out for a walk.'

Vidal sat down and Eva tried not to be so aware of his thigh next to hers. He was wearing trousers and a shirt, sleeves rolled up. No tie. She could see the effect he was already having on the other women in the park.

Eva almost felt defensive. 'It's nice around here. Everyone is so friendly. The barista at the coffee shop knows me by name and I've only been going in for a few days. I worked at the hotel in Madrid for nearly a year and barely anyone knew my name. My boss used to call me Eve.' Then she said, 'I always wanted a dog.'

'The *castillo* could have accommodated a hundred dogs—easily.'

'It wasn't an option. My father hated them, and after he left my mother was in no state to even think about something so frivolous.' She looked at Vidal. 'Were you looking for me for something? We're not going out until later, I thought?'

'Nothing has changed. I just spotted something online that you should see…'

He handed her his phone and Eva looked at it—and went clammy with shock and horror. It was that old picture of her and her father at the event in London a few years ago. Eva was smiling, but still looking like a deer caught in the headlights.

'It was inevitable that they'd dig out anything relevant about you,' Vidal said. 'It seems this was all they could find.' Then he said, 'Eva, look at me.'

Reluctantly she turned her head.

'In the interests of full disclosure, I need to know if there's anything in your past that could come out now.'

Eva handed him back his phone. She felt cold. 'Isn't it a bit late for that?'

He said nothing.

Eva said, 'There is nothing to come out. That was it. The sum total of my socialising.'

'You'll have to explain that to me.'

She glanced at him, and then away again. 'Afraid that it might not square with the narrative you've put together about me in your head?'

Vidal sighed. 'If I have a narrative in my head based on that photograph I don't think it's entirely unfair. It's a pretty damning picture.'

'You've participated in a few damning scenarios of your own,' Eva shot back.

Vidal inclined his head. 'Touché. I had my time going off the rails, I'll admit. Hence the need to make some reparations now.'

Eva looked at him, curious. 'Why did you? Did the money and fame go to your head?'

Vidal grimaced. 'It wasn't as simple as that. It was after my father died. I felt a little…lost for a while. Wondered what it was all for when

I had no one who cared what happened to me.'
His mouth twisted. 'My period of self-pity.'

Eva's heart ached for him. She could understand that feeling of being lost and alone. She said, 'I get it.'

They didn't say anything else for a long moment, and then Eva found the words spilling out of her mouth before she could stop them.

'I went to London not long after your father left the *castillo*, to beg my father to help us. My mother didn't know I'd gone. She would have forbidden me. He met me in his office. I wasn't even invited to his house.' Eva swallowed the pain and bitterness. 'When he saw how desperate I was, he told me that if I did him a favour, he would help. The favour was to accompany him to a party. He put me up in one of the best hotels for the night, and had a stylist come to meet me with an outfit. But when the stylist came she had only that one dress.'

'Go on.'

Eva avoided Vidal's eye. 'The dress was so short I refused to leave the hotel room. But my father came and told me I was making a fuss over nothing, and that if I wanted his help this was what I had to wear. I went with him to the party. At first it seemed okay—I thought I'd been overreacting, even though I still wasn't comfortable in the dress. But then, after a few minutes,

I noticed that it was mostly men. There were other women, but they didn't seem to be wives or girlfriends.'

'They were hired.' Vidal sounded grim.

Eva gasped and looked at Vidal. 'How did you know?'

'Because I've been to parties like that. Not that I've ever stayed.'

Eva felt sick. 'I didn't realise what was happening until my father introduced me to a man and made me go over to a private booth and sit with him. He started touching me. And then he put his hand between my thighs. I didn't think. I just threw my glass of wine into his face. I found my father. I was upset, crying…but he told me that if I couldn't entertain his friend then he couldn't help me.'

'What did you do?'

Eva balked at Vidal's question. 'I left, of course. Went home and said nothing. I haven't seen my father or spoken to him since then.'

Vidal was stony-faced. 'Your father tried to pimp you out?'

'Yes.'

'I'm sorry I misread the situation. I assumed it was a social event with your peers.'

Surprised that he seemed prepared to believe her, Eva felt a warmth bloom in her chest. 'I've never told anyone else about it. I was mortified when that picture appeared online.'

'Your mother never knew?'

Eva shook her head. 'It wasn't long after that that her mental health really started to deteriorate. I had to care for her full-time. Until she died.'

Vidal said nothing for a long moment, and then, 'I assumed that you were making up for lost time—for all those years you were more or less incarcerated at the *castillo* being home-schooled.'

Eva looked away. 'It was a little less exciting than that.'

'So you really haven't been out in society…?'

'No.' Eva forced herself to look at him. 'Maybe that changes your view of the benefits of our… arrangement?'

'I'm a self-made man from a working-class background—no matter what your absence from the social scene might convey, you're still an asset.'

'Even with the dubious company my father keeps?'

'He is unfortunately no different to a lot of men who socialise on that level. It's reprehensible, but it's under the radar.'

'It's disgusting.'

Vidal's jaw clenched. 'It must have been hard to see him like that.'

Eva pushed down the humiliation and the shame. 'I shouldn't have expected anything more.'

Vidal nodded his head towards the playground, where the children were still shrieking and playing. 'I wouldn't have had you down as someone who tolerated children.'

Eva wished that didn't hurt as much as it did. It reminded her of a rare occasion when her mother had taken her out of the *castillo* and into Madrid. They'd found themselves momentarily lost, walking into back streets, with buildings close together. Children had been running freely from one open door to another.

Eva had looked into one house where a family were sitting down to lunch. A baby on its grandmother's knee. A father affectionately scolding a young boy who was running around the table laughing. It had been such an arresting vision that she'd stopped in her tracks and hadn't moved.

Her mother had noticed her fascination and pulled her away sharply, saying, 'You are nothing like them, Eva. You are so much better.'

But she hadn't wanted to be better. She'd envied them.

Eva pushed aside the pang of yearning that

lay underneath the terror she felt at the thought of having children. 'I have no intention of having children. How could I when my own mother barely cared for me?'

'And yet you gravitate to this place?'

She looked at Vidal, wanting his focus off her. He was seeing too much. 'Do you want children?' she asked.

He nodded. 'I've always wanted a family. I was lonely as an only child. My mother couldn't have more after me.'

'I'm sorry. I didn't know that.'

'I'd like at least two or three.'

With the wife he intends to love. Because he believes in love.

All Eva could picture when she thought of love was her mother's bitterness and the cavernous empty rooms of the *castillo*.

Vidal's phone beeped and he looked at it. He stood up. 'I have to go back and take some calls. Santo is preparing lunch.'

'I'll be back shortly.'

Eva watched Vidal leave with his loose-limbed grace. She needed time to absorb their exchange. And the fact that Vidal was so open about wanting love and a family. Alien concepts to her. But they impacted on her so deeply that she felt almost winded.

Vidal was right. She had gravitated here to

enjoy the sights and sounds of happy children playing.

She stood up abruptly and left the park, taking the opposite way to Vidal to walk home the long way.

He was seeing too much, and she was in danger of forgetting her own life lessons. Lessons that told her she had nothing to offer in the way of warm and fuzzy maternal feelings.

To yearn for that was self-indulgent and dangerous, and she put the blame for exposing that weakness squarely on Vidal's shoulders.

'It's an event hosted by the Spanish ambassador to the United States to celebrate Spanish art and culture.'

Eva was in the back of the car with Vidal. She'd just asked about the evening ahead. She was wearing a dramatic strapless black ballgown, complete with a mini train. The hair and make-up team had coiled her hair up into a bun and she wore rubies at her throat and ears. This was evidently the most formal event they'd been to since their debut on the San Francisco social scene almost ten days ago.

Eva had been fooling herself into a false sense of complacency. Telling herself that she was able to resist Vidal's magnetism. But in the past couple of days it had been getting harder and harder.

He hadn't been going into the office, he'd been working at home, and everywhere she turned there he was. As a constant reminder that he wasn't going anywhere.

That this desire wasn't going anywhere.

Eva looked at where her hands rested in her lap, framed by the black silk of the dress. They were soft and clean. Her nails were neatly filed and polished with a gleaming red varnish. Her toenails too.

Vidal had surprised her earlier by getting a manicurist and pedicurist to come to the house before she'd had to get ready. She knew it was only so that she looked the part, but it had felt like a nice gesture.

She held up her hands now and said, 'Thank you for this. I couldn't have done such a good job myself.'

Vidal looked at her hands, devoid of jewellery except for the engagement ring that sparkled in the light.

'You're welcome. As I said, you weren't made to have worker's hands, Eva. I'm just restoring the natural order.'

Putting her back in her place? She chafed at that. 'I think I've proved that I'm not averse to a little manual labour.'

Vidal, resplendent in another classic black tuxedo, inclined his head. 'I'll give you that. I never would have imagined you'd become a chamber-maid.'

Before Eva could think of some witty come-back they were pulling to a stop outside a grand building—one of the city's museums, decked out with a red carpet and lights in the colours of the Spanish flag.

Women in jewel-coloured ballgowns and glittering gems eclipsed the men in their suits as they walked up the steps, framed by flaming lanterns.

Once they were inside, Vidal once again deftly led them through the throng, after handing Eva a glass of champagne. There were typical Spanish tapas being handed out by smiling waiters.

Vidal was soon talking to a couple, and the wife smiled at Eva. She smiled back, conscious of Vidal telling her she didn't smile enough. She'd even tried practising in the mirror one night, until she'd realised she looked ridiculous.

The woman hadn't initiated conversation so Eva was unsure what the protocol was. Then Eva noticed she was wearing a hearing-aid. She put down her glass of champagne and touched the woman's arm. She was about Eva's age. She looked at Eva who signed a few words at her and the woman's face blossomed into a huge smile as she signed back.

You can sign! That's amazing!

Eva made a face and signed, *Not really. Only a little*.

But, together with Eva's rudimentary sign language and some lip-reading, they managed to have a conversation. The woman's name was Sophia and she was there with her husband on a business trip. They lived in New York.

When they left to talk to someone else Eva smiled and waved, buoyed up by the friendly exchange. Sophia had even told Eva to come and visit them in New York.

But then she felt her skin prickle and looked up to see Vidal staring at her as if she had two heads.

'What? Why aren't we moving on? Why are you looking at me like that?'

'Since when can you use sign language? Unless I missed something very fundamental, your mother wasn't deaf. Nor are you.'

A little hurt at his incredulity, Eva said, 'It was a friend at work. My only friend, if you must know. She was partially deaf. She taught me a little. It's really not that hard.'

'Do you have any idea who that was?' Vidal asked.

'Of course not. All I know is that her name is Sophia and she and her husband live in New York. Who are they?'

'He's one of the junior associates in the firm I'm hoping to secure the investment from.'

That sank in. 'Oh…wow. Okay… Did I do something wrong?'

Vidal shook his head. He looked a little shell-shocked. 'On the contrary. He said you were the first person who'd attempted to communicate with his wife. Are there any other skills you've acquired that I should know about?'

Eva felt like giggling at Vidal's reaction. She shook her head. 'Not that I can think of.'

Vidal kept looking at her warily for the rest of the evening, as if Eva was going to suddenly take him by surprise again. She didn't care. She was actually starting to enjoy herself. These events were so much less stuffy than the admittedly few she'd experienced back at home.

And then she heard a familiar beat, and every part of her soul and body went still. *Flamenco*. There was a performance in another room. Like a child following the Pied Piper, Eva followed the distinctive music and stood at the back of the room, watching avidly.

Vidal tugged her forward to sit down, so she had no choice but to follow. She didn't know how long they sat there. She was transfixed. It brought back so many memories of her beloved Maria, and how it was the only thing that had ever really transported her away from the *castillo* and her mother.

I used to watch you.

Vidal. He was watching her now.

She suddenly felt self-conscious, as if her blood was pumping too close to the surface. Beating with too many memories and her desire for him. Flamenco was so elemental it was calling to the most primitive part of her.

She tore her eyes off the show and looked at Vidal, who was still watching her. Sitting back in his seat nonchalantly.

'Sorry, you must have people to talk to. We should get back to the main party. Maybe you should talk to Maria's husband again.'

'If you're sure you don't mind?'

Eva could have stayed there all evening, but she shook her head and stood up. She even smiled. 'No, it's fine.'

Vidal stood up too, and took her hand. Eva wished he wouldn't—especially when she felt so raw.

They went back into the fray. Vidal let go of her hand, but only so he could put his hand on her lower back. It burned through the material of her dress, which suddenly felt very flimsy, even though there were many layers of satin and silk.

By the time they were in the car and heading home Eva felt a little light-headed from everything—the champagne, feeling at ease socially in a way she'd never expected, and from the Flamenco.

Its beat lingered in her blood. She wasn't tired. She was filled with a kind of restless energy. A dangerous energy. Reckless. As if something had shifted this evening. As if a wall had crumbled. An invisible wall that had been holding back her ability to resist Vidal.

Vidal was quiet. The air felt charged between them. Crackling with electricity. Eva tried desperately to tell herself she was imagining it. She was so susceptible to Vidal now, it really wouldn't take much if he wanted to push her into admitting she wanted him.

When they got back to the house Eva slipped off her shoes, and when Vidal said, 'I'm going to have a nightcap on the top floor if you want to join me?' Eva responded far too quickly.

'No. I… No, thank you. I'm tired. I'll go to bed.'

Coward, whispered a voice.

She ignored it. This was self-preservation, not cowardice.

'As you wish. Goodnight, Eva.'

The whole way to her bedroom Eva was wondering why she was fighting her desire. Would it be so bad to give in to Vidal? To let him have his moment of triumph? If it meant that she got to relieve this restless, reckless energy inside her? Was she really so proud?

But when she went into her room something laid out on the bed caught her eye. She went over and realised what it was. She stared at it in disbelief. And then mounting anger. She didn't know how it had appeared like this, but she was becoming used to the life of a billionaire, where you merely thought about something and it manifested.

Here she was, torturing herself, and all the while Vidal was just toying with her. Laughing at her. The poor little rich girl who'd never had any money at all but who had lorded it around the *castillo* like a princess…and then had to get her hands dirty and clean toilets…

And now this.

Eva grabbed what had been left on the bed and marched out of the room to the upper floor, where Vidal was standing with his back to her. Jacket and waistcoat gone. Broad back tapering down to narrow hips and muscular buttocks. The material of his trousers doing little to hide them.

He turned around and she tried not to let his presence distract her. She held up the dress. 'What is this?'

'A Flamenco dress.'

'I can see that.'

'Then why did you ask?'

Eva felt like stamping her foot. 'Why is it in my room?'

'I thought you might like it.'

'Why? Were you hoping for a private show?'

Vidal shrugged, totally unconcerned. 'It's just a gift, Eva. Do what you like with it.'

Eva felt dangerously volatile. 'You want a show? I'll give you a show. And then you can have a good laugh—is that it?'

Without waiting for his response, Eva went back to her bedroom, borne aloft on her anger— an anger she wasn't sure was entirely rational. She couldn't rationalise it. All she knew was that Vidal had always known about one of her deepest most secret things and now he was taunting her with it.

Eva managed to get out of the beautiful ball gown and drape it over a chair. She took off the jewellery she'd been wearing. Then she looked at the Flamenco dress. It was white with black spots and layered frills at the bottom. Classic. She'd always dreamed of owning a dress like this when she'd been teaching herself when she was younger. Maybe that was why she'd had such a visceral reaction.

She put the dress on. It fitted snugly around her chest, waist and hips. The bottom of it felt heavy. She caught it up in one hand and stood tall, with a dancer's straight spine. Her anger had drained away to be replaced by something far more nostalgic.

'It looks good on you.'

Startled, Eva looked at the door, where Vidal was leaning against the frame. He said, 'Try the shoes.'

'There are shoes?' Eva turned around and saw them at the bottom of the bed. Black. She put them on. They fitted perfectly. She said, 'The shoes I had came from Maria—she brought them to the *castillo* for me. I'd outgrown them after a year, but I had to keep using them.'

Vidal said, 'I really didn't mean the dress to be anything other than a gift... After what you told me I ordered it, and it must have arrived while we were out. The timing was a coincidence.'

Eva felt emotional. Vidal was pulling back layer after layer of her past without even realising what he was doing. He was just using her.

And you're just using him...you're still in control... reassured a little voice.

'Will you dance for me?' he asked.

Eva balked, even though moments ago she'd been so angry she'd offered to do just that. 'Now?'

'Why not?'

'But I haven't done it in years.'

'I'm sure it'll come back to you.'

A part of Eva was curious to know if she would remember anything of the painstaking practice she'd used to put in day after day. She felt hot, thinking about Vidal watching her— then and now. About how she'd fantasised about him watching her.

'I… Okay.'

It wasn't as if she could make any more of a fool of herself in front of him.

She followed him back upstairs. The decking on the terrace was the perfect surface for the shoes. Eva walked around, getting used to them. *Heel, toe…toe, heel…* She couldn't look at Vidal, too nervous to see his expression.

She walked around like that for a long moment, and then from somewhere deep inside her came a familiar beat. She didn't need music. It was in her blood. Her soul.

She pulled the dress up and felt her feet take on a familiar rhythm. Slow at first. Deliberate. And then building to a faster beat. She started moving, back and forth. The frills of the dress dropped to the floor and she let herself get lost, exactly as she had done all those years before.

Vidal was mesmerised. As he'd used to be when he'd watched her when she was a coltish teenager, with long, skinny limbs. She'd always been graceful but, when she'd danced she'd taken on a grace that had left him in awe.

She'd used to practise for hours. Over and

over again. Until she was sweating and dizzy. He knew that if he'd made his presence known she would never have forgiven him. He was intruding, but he'd found this other side of her so intriguing. It had been so *counter* to who she was.

And even now, after years of not dancing, Eva was inhabiting the rhythm and the steps in a way that only a true natural talent could. Her body was shaping itself into the traditional Flamenco pose, arched back, arms and hands making elaborate beautiful shapes.

He was almost jealous of the absorption on her face. And that made him shift against the glass railing. He didn't get jealous over women—much less a woman who wasn't even with another man.

The bodice of the dress was cut low enough to display the swells of Eva's breasts. But this wasn't a dance to entice—it was a dance that mocked men for their desire. It was a dance full of the wonder and power of the feminine.

It was the perfect dance for Eva. Mocking him for his desire all over again. Nothing had changed. And he couldn't even blame her this time. He had given her the dress. Asked her to dance.

And now, with each staccato move of her feet and heels, Vidal's control was fraying to pieces.

Eva came to a stop, breathing hard. As if coming out of a trance, she saw Vidal standing a few feet away, arms folded. He looked impossibly stern. Grim. Eva could feel that her hair had come down and was unravelling around her face and shoulders.

She felt undone. The power of the dance still pounded through her blood, as inexpert as she knew she must have been after years of non-practice. She felt powerful, but unsettled, as if she needed something more.

She needed him.

He was the thing that pounded through her body, gathering force. She'd always wanted him. She would always want him.

No, she told herself. That couldn't be. It would be too cruel. *So don't even go there. Protect yourself.*

But Eva feared it was too late already. The time to protect herself had come and gone.

Vidal, as if sensing the need inside her, walked forward, closing the distance between them. Actually, he didn't look grim. She realised he looked *stark*. As if something had been stripped away from him. She felt it too. Exposed. Raw. It resonated deep inside her. A mirroring need.

He said, 'I won't lay a finger on you unless you ask me, Eva.'

Eva couldn't take her eyes off Vidal's mouth. Wide and firm. Beautiful. She wanted to push aside his shirt and run her hands over his chest.

She knew she could turn and walk away. He wouldn't touch her. But the memory of him rejecting her rushed back. She took a step back.

She said, 'What if this is all just a chance for you to humiliate me again? Expose me and then reject me?'

His jaw clenched. 'You were too young, Eva. Too young for what I wanted.'

Without even realising, Eva took a step forward. 'What did you want?'

Vidal's eyes were burning dark aquamarine, like a stormy sea. It was thrilling.

'What I wanted was to kiss you so hard that you wouldn't be able to say another spiteful, nasty word. Until you couldn't breathe. I wanted to bare you to my gaze, bare that body you'd been taunting me with all summer. Cup your breasts in my hands and squeeze the firm flesh. Taste your nipples…bite them. Bite that impudent mouth. I wanted to explore between your legs and feel how much you wanted me.'

His explicit words robbed her of breath, of rational thought.

'I…' She stopped, suddenly nervous. Was she really going to capitulate so easily? Let him have his moment of triumph? Eva knew she wanted Vidal above any other man. The thought of any other man being the first to bare her, touch her, made her skin go cold.

This was no capitulation, even if he thought it was.

This was her salvation.

'Eva, if you're—'

She shook her head. 'No. I'm not. I want this. I want you, Vidal.'

I've always wanted you. From the moment I saw you.

Now Vidal looked wary. 'You're sure?'

Eva tilted her chin up in the way she knew he hated. Arched a brow. 'Maybe you're the one who isn't sure, Vidi?'

Colour slashed along Vidal's cheeks. His mouth thinned. 'Do not call me that.'

'Then make love to me and I won't.'

'Witch,' he growled, as he stepped up close and tugged her towards him, crushed her breasts against his hard chest. He tugged the rest of her hair loose and speared his fingers into the silken mass to cup her head. His other hand clamped firmly on her waist.

She could barely breathe. 'Vidal…please…'

'You're begging…good.'

Before Eva could argue that she wasn't begging, his mouth was on hers and he was kissing her so deeply her legs turned to jelly. He caught her against him, holding her up. Suddenly she didn't care if she was begging. She wanted this.

She lifted her arms up around his neck, straining to get closer. She'd never known a kiss could be so all-consuming. His tongue danced around hers, his teeth finding her lower lip and biting gently.

Her breasts felt full and aching. She moaned softly when Vidal's hand passed over one, cupping the flesh and testing its weight through the thin material of the dress.

Then his hand moved down, and down again, to her thigh. She felt the dress being pulled up until a light breeze danced over her bare skin, and then every part of her blood seemed to flow in a heated rush to between her legs, when Vidal's hand cupped her there.

She gasped and pulled back, dizzy with need. His eyes were so fiery she couldn't look away. His fingers pushed aside her flimsy silk underwear and stroked into her, exploring where she ached most.

Eva could hardly contain the visceral pleasure of Vidal's hand between her thighs. She was shaking with it as his fingers explored deeper, harder. He watched her the whole time, a fierce look on his face. She was panting. She didn't care. She only cared about the ratcheting, tightening spiral of pleasure that was consuming her to the point where she had to cry out as it exploded inside her, sending out waves of pleasure so intense and shocking that she would have fallen if Vidal hadn't caught her up into his arms.

He carried her through the house to his bedroom as Eva floated on a wave of endless little pleasures, before placing her down on the edge of his bed. She looked around dreamily. His room was massive, and dressed in earthy tones. A battered leather armchair in one corner had clothes draped over it. There was a discarded towel on the floor of the en suite bathroom. Curiously intimate details she hadn't expected.

Then she looked up and saw Vidal undoing his shirt. She stood, her limbs still a bit wobbly. She said, 'Wait…let me.'

CHAPTER EIGHT

VIDAL WASN'T SURE how he'd managed to get to his room with Eva in one piece. She was so responsive—in a way that blew his mind. In his deepest fantasies about this woman he'd imagined her being responsive enough to lose all that froideur, but he'd barely touched her and she'd melted into his arms, orgasmed into his hand.

A bell went off in his head even as her fingers got to the bottom of his shirt and he saw he was nearly bared. He caught her hands in his and she looked up at him. It nearly undid him all over again.

Her hair was a wild silken tangle around her face and shoulders. Her mouth was swollen, cheeks pink. Eyes bright.

Exactly how he'd envisaged her. *More*. But he needed to know…

'Eva, wait… When you said you hadn't been out in society much…does that mean that you haven't…been with anyone?'

Even as he asked the question Vidal knew. He saw it in the way she tensed. He should have known from her response just now.

She was looking down, avoiding his eye. He was filled with disbelief, but also a grim sense of confirmation. Everything about this woman was not as he had expected.

Vidal tipped her chin up so she had to look at him. He caught a glimpse of vulnerability before she hid it. He realised how good she was at that. How she had done it before but he'd dismissed it. His guts clenched.

Somewhat defiantly, she said, 'Would it matter if I wasn't experienced? Would you reject me again?'

Vidal shook his head. 'No way. You are not that girl any more.'

She really isn't, a voice prodded him.

He pushed it aside. *Not now*. He couldn't think of that when his whole body was about to go on fire.

'Keep doing what you were doing,' he told her.

She waited a moment, as if not sure what to do, and then she undid the last button on his shirt and spread it open, pushing it off his shoulders and down his arms. He undid the cuffs with economic efficiency and the shirt fell to the floor.

Eva was just looking at him, wide-eyed, and then tentatively she lifted her hands and put them on his chest, fingers spread wide. She was killing him with the most chaste of touches. He would explode if she touched him—

'I used to dream of this,' she said in a low voice. 'I used to watch you…'

'I know.' Vidal knew his voice was dry.

She looked up at him. 'I wanted to talk to you another way…not like I used to…but I didn't know how. I would try…but then I'd see my mother, or she'd call me…and I'd remember I wasn't supposed to be…' She trailed off.

'Treating me like an equal?'

'Something like that.'

He caught her chin and tipped it up. 'We're equals now.'

'Are we?' she asked, and he heard the quaver in her voice. It made his guts clench harder.

He put his mouth to hers—anything to try and keep the focus on the physical. He didn't want to have a conversation with this woman. He just wanted her. But already it felt as if the sand was shifting beneath his feet and he wasn't able to keep his balance.

The kiss deepened. Eva was so sweet… He'd known she'd be sweet under all those tart comments and reprimands. But not as sweet as this. Eager, but reticent. Bold, but shy.

He slowly pulled the zip of her dress down and it loosened around her chest. He moved back and pulled it down her arms. She wore a strapless bra that did little to contain the plump swells of her perfect breasts. The dress fell all the way to the floor, revealing matching underwear. The merest slips of lace.

Vidal was so hard he hurt. Eva stood by the bed. Tall and lissom. Graceful curves. She was a product of her impeccable bloodline, that was for sure. But he couldn't care less about that. He only cared about how they would fit together, and he knew instinctively that they would. In a way that he'd never experienced before.

He walked towards her, undoing his belt as he did so. Her gaze moved lower. He stopped in front of her and pushed his trousers down, stepping out of them. He hooked his fingers into his underwear and pulled that down too, freeing his erection.

Eva's eyes widened, colour slashing her cheeks. Her breasts rose and fell with her breath and he reached for her, turning her around so that he could undo her bra. It floated away. Then he tugged her underwear down and she stepped out of it.

He stood back. He'd been waiting for this moment for a long time. Eva Flores, naked in front of him. Ready to submit to him. Ready to allow him to finally feel a sense of superiority over her.

'Turn around,' he said.

And when she did he felt all of those things, but so much more. She was looking at him, but she had her arms folded over her breasts. His gaze travelled down to the cluster of dark curls hiding her sex.

Dios. How was he going to hold it together enough to even perform? That feeling of superiority was there, because right now in this instance he certainly had more experience, but somehow the sense of superiority was fleeting as he stood in the face of her innocence. An innocence she was trusting *him* with.

The truth was that he felt humbled, and he'd never in a million years expected this. With her.

'Vidal?'

He snapped out of his trance. He saw the slight tremor in Eva's body. She was unsure, and where once he would have revelled in this unexpected twist of events, he found his immediate instinct was to reassure.

He reached for her and pulled her arms down. She bit her lip but didn't look away. Brave. Something else made his gut clench then. Some unnamed emotion.

'You are beautiful.' He felt exposed, so he added, 'But you know that.'

'I don't...not really.'

'Well, you are. Exquisite.'

'So are you.'

He said, 'Lie back on the bed.'

Eva did. Vidal watched her. He came onto the bed beside her and proceeded to indulge all his fantasies, exploring Eva's body, every dip and hollow, and the sharp points of her breasts, until she was moaning, begging and pleading. Incoherent with lust.

Before he lost it completely, he retrieved some protection and rolled it onto his length. He positioned himself between her legs. She looked up at him, full of desire and trust.

He pushed aside the curious ache in his chest and said, 'This might hurt a little, but stay with me. It'll get better, I promise.'

She nodded. Her hands were on his chest. Giving herself to him. He slowly embedded himself in her slick, tight body, sweat breaking out on his brow with the effort it took not to just drive home and explode.

She was more exquisite than anything he'd ever known. It had never been like this before. With any woman. He felt her tense and he stopped. Gritted his jaw. He could feel her body slowly accepting his. Relaxing.

'Okay?' he asked.

She nodded. Eyes wide.

Vidal pushed deeper. And deeper. Until he didn't know where he ended and she began. Then he couldn't move for a long moment, trying to regain control.

Eva shifted under him and he cursed silently.

She said, 'Vidal... I'm okay.'

He felt like huffing a laugh. She might be okay. He wasn't. Amazingly, he felt like a virgin again. With his first woman. Desperately trying not to make a fool of himself.

He moved. Out and back in. Steady long strokes. Letting her get used to him. He reached under her, shifting her up towards him. She gasped when he went even deeper.

Gradually, any restraint was fast unravelling as their movements became faster, more frenetic, and each chased the pinnacle of pleasure. Vidal willed Eva on. She had to come before him.

Her body was sheened with perspiration. She was clutching at him. He could feel the tremors building in her body and as he slammed so deep he saw stars. She went very still, and then it was as if a powerful wave rushed through her entire body, taking him with her as they climaxed together on wave after wave of intense, mind-numbing pleasure.

Vidal slumped over Eva, utterly spent. Her legs were wrapped around his hips. Her body's inner muscles were still pulsating in the aftermath, keeping him deep inside. Keeping him hard. The tips of her breasts scraped against his chest. She was breathing hard.

With extreme effort he lifted his head. 'Okay?'

Dark tendrils of hair were stuck to her forehead. Her cheeks were pink. Her eyes were glazed. Slowly, they focused. She looked at him. She nodded her head jerkily and said, with a rough-sounding voice, 'Is it…always like that?'

Vidal would have loved to have had the wherewithal to say coolly, *All the time.* But, seeing as he was still deeply embedded in her body, and he could barely think straight, he couldn't be anything less than completely honest.

'No…' he said. 'It's rarely like that.'

Eva wasn't sure how long she'd slept. A day? A week? A month? When she woke she was in her own bed, and the curtains were half open. It was bright daylight. Vidal must have brought her back here. She wasn't quite ready to process the meaning of that—beyond the very obvious one that he hadn't wanted to hang out with her after…

Her brain stalled there. *After…* She couldn't totally rationalise what had happened beyond the physical act. She was no longer a virgin. But the taking of her innocence had been such a profound and amazing experience. She'd even asked him if it was always like that. She cringed now.

Maybe he'd brought her back to her own bed because he was embarrassed by her. By her naivety.

Eva groaned under her covers. She was still naked. So Vidal had carried her here naked. After extricating himself from her vice-like grip.

She groaned again.

A robe had been left on the end of the bed. A nice gesture. She sat up and reached for it, groaning again when intimate muscles protested. She went into the bathroom and gasped. She looked a sight. Hair in a wild tangle. Make-up smudged and trailing down her cheeks.

She went cold. Had she cried last night? Tears of ecstasy and joy?

She dived into the shower in a bid to try and scrub away the humiliation. Winced as she found tender spots. Her breasts. Thighs. Between her legs. She could still remember the sheer power of Vidal's body moving into hers. And the quickening, the tightening, that had led to the most extreme pleasure.

No wonder people became sex addicts. She'd only had it once and she was already addicted.

Eventually she came out of the shower, knowing she'd need to face Vidal sooner or later. Hoping he might have gone into the office today, she was dismayed to find him sitting in the informal dining room off the kitchen, having his lunch.

Lunch. She'd slept right through the morning. A pleasure-induced coma. More humiliation.

She took a seat and sat down. Santo appeared with a freshly prepared salad. Eva couldn't meet his eye as she said thank you. She avoided Vidal's eye too. She'd noticed, however, that he was wearing a short-sleeved polo top. And that he looked thoroughly rested. Not as if his life and very being had been turned inside out.

But of course it hadn't. For him it must have been almost—

'How are you?'

Eva nearly dropped her fork. She took a breath. Forced herself to look at Vidal.

He reached over and touched her jaw lightly. 'You have a little burn here. I might have to shave.'

Eva's face went hot. She'd noticed the slight beard rash. Vidal's mark. It was on her skin elsewhere too. She liked it.

'It's fine… I'm fine. Thank you.'

'I didn't go into the office today. I wanted to make sure you were okay… That was intense.'

Some small part of her was slightly reassured to hear him say that. She squinted a look at him. 'It was?'

'Yes, Eva. As much as I'd love to pretend otherwise.'

That reassured her more. If Vidal had been out

to make her feel insecure he wouldn't have had to do much. And she knew that wasn't his style.

She forced herself to eat some salad, even though—amazingly—she didn't have much of an appetite. She couldn't stop the images of last night running through her head. Their hearts pounding in unison. Sweat-slicked skin.

Eva dropped her knife and it fell with a clatter. Vidal had bent and picked it up before she could move. He caught her hand, and she gave up any pretence of trying to eat.

'I think you're afflicted the same way as me,' he said.

She glanced at his plate. Hardly anything eaten either. Vidal's eyes were hot.

A zing of excitement went through her. 'Can we?'

Vidal's fingers intertwined with hers. 'We can do whatever we like.'

He tugged her up to stand and led her from the dining room. Ineffectually, she said, 'But what about lunch…the salads…?'

'We can eat later.'

'We don't have to go out?' Eva was sure that there was an event for them to go to almost every night.

'I've cancelled.'

In Vidal's bedroom, the bed had been remade. Eva's dress was hanging up on the back of a door. She blushed when she saw it. There was no sign of her underwear.

Vidal said from behind her, 'Are you sore?'

Eva turned around. She felt shy. She shook her head. 'Just a little tender.'

Vidal came close and caught a lock of her hair, twining it around his finger, tugging her closer. 'Remember when I said there were plenty of places to kiss you other than on your mouth?'

Eva's breath hitched. She nodded.

'Well, take off your clothes and lie back on the bed, because I'm going to show you exactly what I meant.'

Hours later, Vidal stood by the bed. It was dark outside. Eva was on her front, a sheet pulled up over her bottom, her back long and elegant. An arm up by her face.

He had intended on going to work that morning. But when Eva hadn't appeared for breakfast he'd given in to an impulse to stay at home. He'd told himself it was just to make sure she was okay. Because last night had been…unprecedented. And not just because she'd been a virgin.

It had surpassed Vidal's wildest fantasies. When he'd finally come back to consciousness Eva had been deeply asleep, and he'd found himself watching her for a long time. On some level, he'd been marvelling at what had happened. The fulfilment of so much.

She'd been a virgin.

At every step of the way since he'd met her again she'd confounded Vidal's expectations. The truth was that he thought he'd known her... but in fact did he know her at all?

The lure of leaving her in his bed had been so strong that he'd moved her back to her own bed. She'd barely stirred. His conscience had pricked at the thought of her waking alone, but then he'd reminded himself that he didn't do cosy mornings-after with lovers.

She's different.

Precisely, he'd told himself. All the more reason to make sure there was no ambiguity about her role.

So then he'd told himself he'd wait till lunch. Make sure she was okay and then go to work. But then she'd appeared, and Vidal had known he wasn't going anywhere.

Within minutes he'd been leading her back to the bedroom, and for the first time in his working life he'd blown off meetings to indulge his desires. Indulge in an afternoon of unabated sybaritic pleasure. When even through his wildest days Vidal had never pursued pleasure over work.

Eva was an intoxicating mix of novice and

practised seductress. One minute she'd had him doubting that she had even been a virgin, and the next she'd been blushing from her feet up to her neck.

Once again, Vidal didn't want to move her. He wanted to climb into the bed beside her.

So he moved her. Back to her own bedroom. She barely woke, and he ignored his conscience. Again.

Had another week gone by? Had two? Eva wasn't even sure. She was in some kind of limbo land, where she would wake late, eat, read or swim, or take a walk to the park, and then Vidal would come home, they'd go out and then, within the most respectable amount of time possible, would leave whatever event they were at and come home and—

Eva blushed now, just remembering the previous night.

She pulled her knees up under her chin, sitting on one of the luxurious seats on the top terrace area.

They had barely made it into the house from the car. They hadn't made it to the bedroom. They'd made love on the first floor, clothes strewn along the way like teenagers.

Eva had got up very early to retrieve them, before Michael or Santo could find evidence of their lust. The staff didn't live in the house, but they arrived quite early each day.

She had also got up early because it had been clear since that first night that Vidal had no intention of allowing Eva the indulgence of sleeping in his bed all night. Until morning. Like regular lovers. That was okay, she'd told herself. It actually helped her to keep a certain amount of perspective and distance, even if both perspective and distance faded to dust as soon as she looked at Vidal.

At least one of them was experienced in that regard. And she could appreciate those strong boundaries because in so many other ways she was losing it…

Eva buried her head in her knees. Vidal didn't have to tell her to smile any more because she couldn't stop. She felt so much lighter. As if a burden had been lifted off her shoulders. For the first time in her life she felt her age. She felt young and free and as if her whole life was waiting for her.

It is, reminded a voice. *Without Vidal. Don't forget why you're here.*

Eva's smile faded. She hadn't forgotten the genesis of this agreement. The fact that Vidal had felt a certain need for retribution. To make her pay for her youthful transgressions. But in the last few days it felt as if something had changed. As if they'd moved on from that. As if…

As if what? As if you're in a real relationship with a man who has already told you that he will marry for love and that you are the last woman he would marry?

Eva scowled now. She hadn't forgotten that. But it felt as if they were finally communicating in the way that Eva had always dreamed of when she was younger. Conversing. As equals.

She heard a noise at that moment and looked around. Vidal was striding out onto the terrace, jacket off, tie gone, shirt open at the throat, holding a glass of what looked like whisky.

Eva sat up straight. 'Hi…' She felt shy around him all the time now.

Vidal said, 'Hi, yourself. Good day? Do you want a drink?'

Eva tried not to be put off by Vidal's breezy nonchalance. She wasn't used to this situation. How to act with a lover.

She nodded, 'Fine, thanks—and, no, I'm okay for a drink.'

It had been an amazing day. She'd gone to the park, had a coffee. Come back, read one of Vidal's books from his library. She'd allowed herself to daydream about her future… But she held all that back, still not completely at ease with divulging everything in her head.

She stood up. 'Actually, I spent the afternoon slaving over a hot stove to make us dinner.'

She ignored Vidal's nonplussed expression and went down to the kitchen, aware of him following her, and suddenly aware of the fact that she was wearing soft sweats and a loose shirt. Hair in a messy bun.

She stopped and turned around. Vidal was right behind her. She gestured to her clothes. 'I'm taking advantage of the fact that we're not going out tonight. Is that okay?'

'It's completely fine. This house is your home too, for as long as you're here.'

For as long as you're here.

Eva's heart hitched. She wasn't imagining him putting down boundaries—they were so clear they could be marked with flashing lights and police tape.

In the kitchen, she pressed a button on the state-of-the-art oven. She said brightly, 'It'll just take a minute to heat it up.'

There was bread and salad, covered over, on the counter.

Vidal put down his glass. 'What is "it"?'

'A chicken casserole with a little twist, I added some harissa—'

'I've eaten already.'

She stopped. 'Oh. You didn't mention you would.'

'Should I have?'

'Well, no… I guess I just assumed that you'd want to eat in as we weren't going out.'

Eva was ravenous for a home-cooked meal. They hadn't eaten a proper dinner in days—just bits of food at various events.

'And so you cooked?'

Eva was starting to feel a tingle of irritation at Vidal's reaction. It was as if she'd done something outrageous. 'Yes. I can cook. I like to cook. Hence, dinner.'

'Since when do you cook?'

'Since I had to, or my mother and I would have gone hungry. Maria taught me how to bake when I was small.'

'Where's Santo?'

'I said he could go home. It's his partner's birthday.'

'Well, like I said, I've eaten already. But you go ahead. I have to make some calls.'

He picked up his glass and was just turning to go when Eva reacted impulsively and picked up a piece of bread and threw it at him. It bounced off his shoulder. He stopped and turned around. Eva felt like giggling—but also not.

'What was that for?'

She lifted her chin. 'For being rude. You could have had the courtesy to tell me you'd be eating out. Every evening I'm expected to trot along in your wake, to every envelope-opening in the city. The one evening we have off, I thought it would be nice to eat a home-cooked meal.'

Vidal came back over to the counter. 'I'm not in the business of "home-cooked meals".'

Eva folded her arms. 'Maybe when you get married you will be.' She cursed herself inwardly for mentioning marriage.

'I most likely will. And I'm sure I'll enjoy them.'

'But not with me?'

'No. Because our relationship is not about that.'

'Oh, I'm sorry—have I strayed over the invisible boundary marking our relationship?'

'I have a chef and a housekeeper. You're not here because I need either of those things.'

'So what you're saying is that you couldn't care less about me as a person—you're just interested in me as a trophy and for sex.'

Eva felt ridiculously hurt, even though Vidal had never been anything but brutally honest about that. The way she'd been mooning over Vidal just a short while before, telling herself that maybe they'd transitioned to a better place, mocked her.

She said, 'You accused me of not being a nice person, Vidal—but you know what? *You're* not being very nice right now. In fact, you're being a complete—'

Vidal moved so fast he took the word out of Eva's mouth and replaced it with his mouth on hers. Like a brand. Fiery and irresistible.

She was responding before she could stop herself. And then she pulled back, disgusted. 'What are you doing?'

Vidal's eyes were bright, his jaw tight. 'Reminding us both of why we're here.'

'A business deal with benefits and a side of revenge. I remember now. Thank you.' Eva's voice was bitter.

'Damn it, Eva. We're not here to play house. I'll do that with my wife.'

Eva smirked to hide her pain—because the pain she was feeling was indescribable, and it shouldn't be. 'What if you fall in love with someone who doesn't want to play house or cook for her husband?'

'If I love her it won't matter,' Vidal gritted out. 'After all, it's not as if I can't afford to have staff to do all that.'

'I *really* don't like you right now.'

'I don't need you to like me.'

The energy between them was volatile. Crackling with electricity. A short time before Eva had been hungry and looking forward to eating. Now she'd lost her appetite. Another appetite had taken over. Lust. And anger. And a desire to punish Vidal for being so cool and for mentioning his future *wife*.

She pressed a button on the oven and turned back to Vidal. She started undoing her shirt. Which was actually his shirt. She'd worn his shirt like some love-sick girlfriend. Angry with herself as much as him, she tore it off and threw it to the ground.

Vidal's eyes flared with heat when he took in the fact that she wasn't wearing a bra. He breathed out. 'Now we're on the same page...'

He came over and lifted Eva up with effortless strength onto the island in the centre of the kitchen. He spread her legs wide and moved between them. She could feel the heat of his arousal against her, and as he bent his head and surrounded the hard tip of one breast in hot, wet heat, she knew she could exult in this at least. Her effect on him. There was no doubt about that.

She just had to remember that he was only interested in seeing her either on her back, or by his side dressed in couture.

When Vidal woke in the morning the sun was up. He felt disorientated. He was usually up much earlier. His body felt heavy and replete.

Sated. Yet still hungry. A sensation he'd only experienced with Eva.

Eva.

The bed beside him was empty. It usually was when he woke. It was as if she'd taken the hint after that first night, when he'd taken her back to her own bed, and now she left before he woke.

It should have pleased him. But he found it unsettling. As if the fact that she was doing it irked him somehow. Which was ridiculous and contrary. *He* was the one who'd made sure she didn't get any ideas.

Did a part of him want to wake up and find her nestled beside him, their legs entwined? *Perhaps*, he told himself angrily, throwing the covers back, *but only so he could make love to her again.*

As he stood under the steaming shower a few seconds later he tried not to think of the previous evening, but he couldn't help it. Eva was right—he'd been rude. Rude in a way that he wouldn't accept from anyone. Rude in a way he wouldn't have accepted from her.

For years he'd taken her to task for her rudeness. But last night it had been him. Because when he'd walked through the house, for the first time he'd noticed little things. Additions. Evidence of the presence of a woman.

Her shoes by the door—the sandals that she'd

worn that day, presumably to the park. Flowers on the reception table. He never bought flowers. Bright, vivid blooms. They reminded him of his mother. She'd always had flowers in their apartment, no matter how broke they'd been. A shawl on the back of a couch in the TV lounge. A book left open on a coffee table.

The markers of someone else in the house. Not altogether unwelcome. The kind of things he would have expected of a partner. *A wife*. Not a temporary lover.

So when he'd found Eva on the terrace, in soft sweats that clung to her long shapely legs and one of his shirts, hair down and looking sexier than anything he'd ever seen in his life, he'd found it intensely provocative. Even when she hadn't even been trying to be provocative. Or maybe she had and he was the fool.

He'd reacted to her having cooked dinner like a total boor. But it had pushed him over the edge. The edge of not knowing how to handle *this* Eva. The one who surprised him and confounded him at every turn. The Eva who'd worn her vulnerability on her sleeve for the first time. The Eva who had allowed him to take her innocence but had taken the hint and now went back to her own bed.

Vidal emitted a curse and shut off the shower. Even just thinking of her had his body reacting.

His libido was out of control and it didn't seem to be on the wane. Very much the opposite.

A prickle of panic caught at his gut. He should be wanting her less by now. That was usually the way with a lover. Actually, usually he lost interest far sooner. But with Eva he'd allowed himself to believe that their shared past and all she had put him through had added a level to their relationship that put it outside of what he considered normal.

Vidal threw on some jeans and a shirt. He walked past Eva's bedroom and glanced inside. The bed was neatly made and the sun was shining in. This sign of order irked him.

He found her in the kitchen. She was wearing a long button-down dress. Simple but sexy. Hair pulled back and in a loose plait to keep it out of her way. He knew she knew he was there, because she'd tensed.

That irked him too.

'I owe you an apology,' he said.

Eva stopped what she was doing with Tupperware bowls and looked at Vidal. 'For what?'

'You made dinner and I was rude.'

Eva looked away and shrugged. 'It's fine. I should have sent you a message. I shouldn't have assumed you'd want to eat here. You have your routine.'

'What are you doing?'

Eva placed a lid on a plastic bowl. 'I'm packing up the food from last night for Santo—he has an arrangement with a charity for the homeless to donate anything left over or unused.'

'Oh.' Vidal felt off-kilter. Why didn't he know that? How did Eva know that? And since when did she care about charity?

It was very clear to Vidal that things had veered way off course, and without pondering his decision he knew exactly what he had to do now, to be able to put this episode behind him so they could both move on.

It was time to get Eva out of his system.

CHAPTER NINE

'You want to go where?' Eva looked at Vidal disbelievingly.

'My house in Hawaii. Maui, to be precise.'

Eva was still absorbing the fact that he'd apologised for turning down dinner last night. She thought he'd made up for it by ravishing her to within an inch of her life. It had taken extreme effort for her to get out of his bed before he'd woken to find her there.

'Forgive me if I'm wrong,' Eva said carefully, 'but I'm pretty certain that a tropical island isn't in the guidebook for fake engagement relationships.'

Although the thought of being in a tropical paradise with Vidal was…intoxicating.

'I need to go and check on some maintenance issues, and some friends are having a party there. It's just for a few days.'

'I… Do I have a choice?'

'You always have a choice, Eva,' Vidal said.

But she knew she didn't. Not really. It wasn't as if she'd ever be going to a place like that with Vidal again. The weak part of her that she was slowly embracing and learning not to see as a negative thing begged her just to give in. What harm could it do? She was already in so deep with this man…

So Eva feigned as much nonchalance as she could and shrugged lightly. 'Sure, it sounds nice. When do we leave?'

'Within the hour.'

All nonchalance was gone. Eva squeaked, 'An *hour*?'

They arrived in Maui when it was still daylight, as Hawaii was three hours behind San Francisco. It was a lush green paradise and Eva had never been anywhere like it.

A car and driver met them and drove them to Vidal's property high in the hills, with spectacular views down to the sea. Eva got out of the car and stood taking in the view. Vidal came to stand beside her.

She shook her head. 'This is…breathtaking.'

Vidal took her hand. 'Come on, I'll show you around.'

Eva let him lead her into the beautiful white wooden house perched on the top of this idyllic hill. Dark wood floors gleamed to a high shine.

The windows were all open, allowing a breeze to flow through, muslin curtains fluttering gently. The furniture was simple, rustic, but it looked comfortable. The kitchen was massive, and the dining room was just inside some tall French doors, with another dining area on the outdoor terrace. There was an infinity swimming pool in the garden below, surrounded by flowering bushes.

An iridescent bird flew through the house and Eva gasped.

Vidal said, 'You'll get used to it. The wildlife here makes itself at home.'

He led her upstairs to the bedrooms, all decked out with en suite bathrooms and the same dark wood flooring. Bright rugs. Massive beds dressed in crisp cotton.

To Eva's horror, she felt emotional. This place was like somewhere she'd dreamed of but hadn't realised it till now. Tears stung her eyes, and to her horror, Vidal noticed.

'Hey, are you okay?'

Eva shook her head quickly and took her hand out of his. 'Fine…just got a speck of dust or something in my eye.'

Vidal curled his hand into itself. Maybe this had been a mistake. For a second he'd have sworn Eva was crying. And he could understand how she felt, because when he'd first come here he'd felt emotional too.

He'd intended on this being an almost surgical operation. Bring Eva here, sequester her in his house and gorge himself on her until she was finally out of his system. Pure sex.

But they'd only just arrived and it already felt as if he was fast losing control of the situation.

He moved back. 'This is your room. I'm down the hall.'

Eva avoided his eye. She went to the doors that led out to a balcony. 'It's beautiful...thank you.' Her voice was husky.

Vidal's gut twisted. He was about to ask her if she was okay again, but then a voice came from downstairs.

'Yoo-hoo! Anyone home?'

Eva turned around from the balcony doors. What was wrong with her? Almost blubbing all over Vidal because of the spectacular views and the peace of the place?

A woman had appeared in the bedroom doorway, with a massive smile on her face. She greeted Vidal warmly, with a kiss and a hug. Eva felt self-conscious. Too stiff for this relaxed place.

Vidal was saying, 'Chelle, meet Eva Flores—Eva this is Chelle, my friend, intrepid housekeeper, chef and general busybody, who doesn't hesitate to dish out life lessons at every opportunity.'

Eva felt ridiculously shy in the face of the other woman's natural easy-going effervescence. It was if she was realising that all the loosening up she had done since coming to America with Vidal was just a drop in the ocean of how far she needed to go.

She stuck out a hand, tried to smile, but it felt forced. She could feel herself pulling back the old armour that had protected her for so long.

'So nice to meet you, Chelle.' She winced. She sounded so stuffy.

The woman's clasp was warm and firm. Her dark eyes so kind that ridiculously Eva almost felt like crying again.

She let Eva's hand go and said briskly, 'I've left some snacks downstairs, and I'll be back later to do dinner. Hal will be over first thing in the morning, to go over the jobs that need doing.' She looked at Eva and explained, 'Hal is my husband.'

'And they've just welcomed baby number three to their brood.'

Vidal was smiling. No doubt already imagining his own brood some day. The thought made Eva feel even more wobbly.

She said, 'Congratulations. A boy or a girl?'

Chelle smiled. 'A girl. We've called her Lucy.'

'You'll meet them all at the party,' said Vidal.

Eva looked at him. 'Party?'

'It's Hal's fortieth this weekend. That's the party I mentioned.'

'Oh, of course...'

Eva had assumed it was going to be another formal society party. Not a friends' party. This was nearly more frightening to her than the other kind. She was only just getting used to navigating that world. And now she was going to be thrown into another one.

Except, as much as she'd dreaded the society world, at least she'd had some sort of template for it. But parties in the real world? With relatively normal people? She didn't have a clue.

'This food is delicious,' Eva said appreciatively.

And it was. Chelle had left out a veritable feast of cold meats and cheeses, bread and salads. Gazpacho soup. Crisp white wine.

She and Vidal were sitting at the island in the kitchen, the warm breeze flowing around them and bringing scents from the garden.

'Why did you buy property here?' Eva asked impulsively.

'Why not? It's beautiful, as you can see.'

Eva rolled her eyes. 'Yes, but why here specifically?'

'My mother always talked about coming to Hawaii. Her dream was to go on a cruise with my father when they retired and see the world. Hawaii, for some reason, was one of the places she always spoke about.'

'Did they ever come here?'

Vidal laughed. 'They never left Spain. That's why my mother pushed me so hard,' he went on. 'She knew I was intelligent enough to do something. To get out of Spain and see the world.'

'She sounds like she was a formidable woman.'

'She was.'

Eva remembered seeing something on the way in. 'That's why you called the house Casa Inez? After your mother?'

Vidal nodded. 'Yes.'

'That's a lovely tribute to her. I'm sorry she didn't get to see this place.'

'Me too.'

'I can't imagine wanting to name anything after *my* mother.'

Eva saw Vidal's sharp look.

'You're not sorry she's gone?'

Eva looked at him. Shocked. 'Of course I'm sorry she's gone… I loved her.' She bit her lip. 'But truthfully… I can't say I didn't feel a sense of…liberation. Our relationship was complicated. We were all we had. I can see now how unhappy she was…how it affected her mental health. She was pretty much agoraphobic in the end. She wouldn't leave the *castillo* no matter what. Not even to get medical treatment when she had pains in her chest. I called the paramedics, but by the time they came it was too late. She'd had a heart attack and died.'

'I didn't know that. It must have been traumatic.'

Eva tried not to think of the sheer panic she'd felt. 'It was. I did a course in CPR after she died. I never want to feel so helpless again. What if I could have saved her?'

To her surprise, Vidal took her hand. She looked at him.

He said, 'I know what it's like to watch a loved one die and I know there's nothing you can do.'

'Thank you.'

A moment shimmered between them. Light and delicate. Then Vidal took his hand away and said, 'I'm afraid I have to make a couple of quick calls in the study, but you should explore and rest. Lie by the pool.'

Eva smiled. 'That sounds good.' In truth, she'd welcome a little respite—a chance to get her bearings.

Just before he left, though, Vidal turned at the door. 'Were you okay earlier? You seemed a little off with Chelle?'

'Oh, no!' Eva said, genuinely dismayed. 'It's

just…sometimes I'm not sure how to behave around people. She seems so lovely and friendly.'

'She is. She has no agenda. She's one of the most genuine people I know. Everyone here is the same.'

Vidal walked out and Eva couldn't help but feel that it had been some kind of warning: *Behave with my friends.*

He still didn't trust her.

And it shouldn't matter. But it did.

When Vidal emerged by the pool as the sun was setting he took in the view. The view of Eva lying face-down on the lounger. She wore a one-piece. Disappointing. He made a mental note to burn all one-piece swimsuits. Her skin was glistening with sun cream. Lightly golden. Her hair was pulled back and caught up in a bun, exposing her neck.

Vidal dropped his towel onto the lounger beside her and sat down. She opened her eyes. Dark and golden. Amazing to think that once he'd thought them cold and now all he thought of when she looked at him was heat.

She came up on one elbow. She looked deliciously sleepy. 'What time is it?'

'About five. Chelle is going to be back in an hour to get dinner ready.'

Eva turned and sat up. 'Okay, I'll get ready.'

Vidal reached for her, tugging her over onto his lounger, making her squeal. 'Not yet. I have plans for the next hour.'

She was breathless. 'You do?'

'Yes.'

She had her back to him and he slipped a hand between one swimsuit strap and her shoulder, to push it down her arm. The next one followed. He tugged the material all the way down, baring her breasts. He cupped them, testing their firm weight, his fingers trapping her nipples.

Eva moaned and arched her back. She reached behind her for Vidal, who was wearing only board shorts. Her hand finding his hardness and cupping him. Teasing him.

He stood up and pulled her with him. Quickly he dispensed with his own shorts and her swimsuit until they were both naked. Eva giggled. It almost stopped Vidal in his tracks. He'd never heard her giggle. She seemed almost surprised by it herself, putting a hand over her mouth.

He said, 'Do you know how many fantasies I used to have of you in that pool at the *castillo*?'

Eva shook her head. He took her hand and led her to the steps leading down into the pool.

Eva still felt a little hazy from her nap as Vidal led her down into the deliciously cool water. The sky was turning to violet around them. The night chorus of birds was starting up. She wondered if in fact she was Eve and he was Adam. It felt primeval at this moment, as the silky water caressed their bodies and Vidal took her deeper and deeper until she couldn't stand and she had to put her legs around his waist.

She allowed herself to fall all the way into the dream. The dream that this was real and that Vidal loved her as much as she loved him.

It was only later, when Eva was back in the bedroom, her whole body still tingling after what had happened in the pool, that she acknowledged what had gone through her mind in that dream-like moment.

She loved Vidal.

But that was crazy. She didn't even know what love was. How could she? What she'd experienced from her mother had been some sort of toxic love. And no one else had ever loved her. Apart from maybe the housekeeper Maria.

So it couldn't be love. It was infatuation. Lust-induced emotion. That was it.

Vidal certainly didn't love her. He would fall about laughing if he knew that, of all things, she'd actually fallen for him.

The ultimate revenge.

She pushed the notion of love out of her head and gave herself a quick once-over. She was wearing a strappy red maxi-dress. Sandals. Hair down. Face scrubbed clean. She loved not having to dress up.

Vidal was nowhere to be seen in the kitchen, but Chelle was there. She saw her, and Eva apologised.

Chelle smiled and said, 'Don't be silly—come in…help me. There are some mushrooms waiting to be chopped on the board.'

Delighted to be given something to do so she didn't have to navigate a conversation, Eva smiled. 'Yes, please.'

But Chelle was so friendly and open and easy that it was impossible not to just follow her lead and engage in conversation. Without even realising it, Eva found she was telling her about the *castillo* and her mother.

Chelle looked at her at one point. 'That place sounds crazy—like something out of a gothic novel.'

Eva shrugged, self-conscious. 'I mean, it was amazing… I was very privileged.' How many times had Vidal levelled *that* accusation at her?

Chelle surprised her by squeezing her arm gently. 'It sounds like it was amazing, but not very…homely.'

Eva laughed out loud at the notion, and then put her hand to her mouth as if she was surprised at the sound. She shook her head. 'No, not homely at all. The opposite, in fact.'

The conversation flowed and Chelle poured some wine for Eva. She didn't even notice Vidal standing in the doorway until he said, 'That's quite enough fraternising with the staff.'

Chelle looked up and threw a piece of raw green pepper at Vidal, who caught it deftly and promptly ate it.

She said, 'Don't worry. Thanks to my commis chef here, dinner is ready and I will take my leave.'

Chelle waved goodbye to Eva, who was genuinely touched by the woman's warmth and humour.

Eva had already laid the table outside on the terrace and lit candles. She brought out the plates of food and the wine. Vidal was in a crisp white shirt and faded jeans. Mouthwateringly sexy.

'You didn't have to help prepare dinner,' he said as they sat down.

'I didn't mind. I told you—I enjoy cooking. Although I'm nowhere near Chelle's level of proficiency.'

'She's a trained chef.'

'So she was telling me.' Eva swallowed a delicious mouthful of seafood risotto and a sip of wine and then said, 'You don't cook?'

'I never had to, really. I was either in boarding school then at university or at the *Castillo* with my father. And at university I ate like everyone else—terribly.'

'And then you made your millions, so you could always afford to hire a chef.'

Vidal drank some wine. 'Something like that...'

They were silent for a moment, and then Eva put down her fork. The night around them was soft and dark, like a cocoon. 'You know... I envy you.'

Vidal put a hand to his chest, '*You*, the princess of the *castillo*, envy *me*?'

Eva felt a dart of hurt. 'Don't call me that, please.'

He picked up his glass and said, 'Noted.'

She clinked her glass with his. 'Thank you.'

'So tell me: why do you envy me?'

'Your opportunity to go to university... I always wished for that.'

'You could have gone.'

Eva shook her head. 'Apart from no money, I wasn't bright, like you. I wouldn't have got a scholarship. I left traditional school at the age of twelve. My home-school tutor was a joke. I'd probably barely have scraped through the most basic exams.'

'Lots of people have only a rudimentary education and go on to university.'

'Perhaps… I wanted to do a degree in business and economics.'

'There's nothing stopping you now. It's just a matter of putting in the work to get the basic qualifications. I would give you the money to do that, Eva.'

She looked at Vidal, horrified. 'I didn't tell you for that reason…you don't have to give me anything. You've done enough. Not everything has to be a transaction.'

Vidal sat back. 'I'm sorry. I didn't mean it like that. But it's a very achievable dream, Eva.'

Slightly mollified, she said, 'Sorry, I overreacted. I just don't want you to think I'm grasping for whatever I can get.'

Vidal sat forward again and shook his head. 'Believe me, you're the least mercenary woman I've ever met.'

Eva smiled and held up a finger. 'Ah, one positive quality in my favour!'

Vidal's eyes gleamed like two aquamarine jewels. 'Oh, you have a few more, don't worry.'

Eva blushed. Ridiculously. She hated it that she craved his approval so desperately.

Vidal looked at Eva in the flickering candlelight. He knew he'd never seen a woman as beautiful. And might not ever again. But there was something even more to her beauty now—a kind of luminescence that had never been there before. She didn't look so serious. So pensive. So… haughty.

In fact, just now, when he'd found her in the kitchen with Chelle, helping, he'd felt like saying, *Would the real Eva Flores please stand up?*

Half idly, he said now, 'Who are you, Eva? Are you this person who really likes to cook and dress down and who isn't remotely mercenary?'

She looked at him, startled. 'What do you mean?'

He waved a hand between them. 'You bear little resemblance to the girl I knew. The one who wanted to slap me in a fit of pique.'

Eva's eyes were dark tonight. He couldn't read them.

Eventually she said, 'Is it so hard to believe that I've changed?'

'Changed dramatically. To the point where I'm wondering if this is all some kind of an elaborate ruse.'

He saw her fingers tighten on her glass.

'To what end, Vidal?' she asked.

'To lull me into a false sense of security?'

'What? So that I can have my wicked way with you? I think that horse has already bolted. And you were the one intent on seducing me, remember?'

'It didn't take much seduction in the end.'

Eva stood up, clearly agitated. She walked over to the terrace railing, her back to Vidal. He couldn't fully understand it but he felt the need to push her...to try and get her to reveal something.

She turned around and her face looked...stark. 'Why are you doing this?' she demanded.

'Because I learnt a long time ago with you never to trust these kinds of moments. Because you'll always come back with some zinger or put-down.'

'Maybe I'm all out of zingers and put-downs.'

Vidal could see that her eyes were shining. With emotion?

This was too much. Who did she think she was kidding?

He stood up and went over to her. She stood with her back against the railing, hands by her hips.

'What's your problem, Vidal?'

There she was. The Eva he knew. Even if she wasn't quite as sharp as he remembered.

He came close, until he could see the golden lights in her eyes.

'My problem is why you think you need to put on this act. It's to no end, Eva. Nothing else is going to happen here. We'll be going our separate ways very soon. There won't be any permanent arrangement.'

Her mouth twisted. 'Permanent arrangement? Since when did you get so arrogant? You told me that I'm the last woman you'd want to marry. Well, don't worry, Vidal, because you are literally the last man I would marry.'

She put a hand to his chest and pushed, but he placed a hand over hers. 'That's all I wanted to say, Eva. Just that you don't need to put in this effort, pretending to be something you're not.'

She looked up at him. 'What if this is who I am, Vidal? What if the girl you knew was the one who was putting on a front and pretending to be someone she wasn't just to survive? Have you ever considered that?'

She took her hand from under his and walked around him and into the house. For the first time in his life Vidal was not sure he knew which way was up any more. And if what she'd just said was true, then the very basis of everything he believed was suddenly in doubt.

'I'm sorry.'

Eva didn't look up from the book she was not reading. She was so hurt and so angry with Vidal that she was trembling with it. His legs and feet came into her line of vision. She hadn't realised he was barefoot. He had very beautiful but very masculine feet.

Her pulse tripped. Damn him anyway.

He tugged the book out of her hand and looked at it, reading out the title. '*The Tech Revolution*. I don't recommend it—it's very dry.' He threw it aside.

He came down on his haunches in front of her. Eva refused to look at him. She felt like a petulant child.

'Eva. Please look at me. I'm sorry.'

She looked at him and hoped her hurt wasn't visible on her face. She said, 'I can't keep apologising for the past, Vidal. I know you can't understand it, and I'm not even sure that I can fully, yet, but I was always aware of how I was behaving. I just didn't know how to be any other way. My mother's presence…her influence…was so pervasive. It isn't an excuse for my behaviour, which I know was atrocious. I'm just simply trying to explain…'

Vidal said, 'The truth is that it doesn't matter, and I shouldn't have brought it up. Because we're not here to talk about the past or even who we are now. We're together for a finite amount of time, and the sooner this chemistry between us burns out, the sooner we can get on with our lives.'

Even now, when he'd hurt her and was basically telling her that he didn't care to find out the truth about who she really was, Eva felt the pull to just cleave to him. To tell him with her body who she was, even though he wouldn't notice.

She made a split-second decision. If he could be so cold, then so could she. She would surround herself in ice—it wasn't as if she didn't have practice.

Eva stood up, and Vidal rose fluidly too. She walked to the door and he said from behind her, 'Where are you going?'

She looked at him over her shoulder. 'You mean you don't already know? You seem to know everything else.' She pushed one strap of her dress down one shoulder. 'This chemistry isn't going to burn itself out, now, is it?'

She sauntered out of the room, pushing the other strap down her shoulder. By the time she was at the stairs, the dress was down to her waist. Granted, it didn't take Vidal long to gather his wits, but it had been a very satisfying few seconds catching him off guard.

He recovered soon enough, taking Eva into his arms before she could protest. The grim look on his face secretly thrilled her—because she knew she was getting under his skin.

Good.

Because he was so deep under her skin that she dreaded to think of the day when he would look at her with no interest and she would have to confront her true feelings about him.

Not now. Not yet. Not ever.

'But I've never held a baby!'

'It's like riding a bike…or something,' Chelle said as she handed her baby girl into Eva's tense arms.

Eva had no choice but to hold the baby because Chelle was gone, tending to something for the party.

It was on the beach. A very relaxed and casual affair. Music playing from huge speakers. Flaming lanterns. Tables stuffed with delicious food. Drinks.

Everyone was so friendly and happy. Eva's fears had been quashed straight away, and there was no time to be nervous or worry about how to act or what to say.

She and Vidal had arrived late. Since the other day there had been a kind of fierceness between them. They didn't have conversations. They looked at each other and within minutes they were in bed. Her bed or his—it didn't matter.

That morning, when she'd woken in his bed, she'd made a move to get up, but he'd caught her back and whispered sleepily into her neck, 'Don't go. Stay.'

She'd lain there under his arm for what had felt

like aeons. She'd known he hadn't really wanted her to stay, so eventually she'd managed to sneak out and back to her room.

Hal, Chelle's husband, had been at the house the past couple of days, giving Eva a chance to get some space and also to watch Vidal work on the house with him—in shorts, shirtless… The memories of watching him covertly at the *castillo* had been vivid and bittersweet.

But now she was sitting here, terrified, with a live, wriggling bundle of vulnerable flesh in her arms. She was almost afraid to breathe.

The little girl let out a squawk and Eva looked up, but no one was around. She tried jiggling the baby the way she'd seen Chelle do it, so effortlessly, while holding a plate in the other hand and with a toddler clinging to her leg. Miraculously, the baby stopped squirming and opened her eyes. Eva gasped. They were dark brown. Long lashes. In spite of her terror and fear she was mesmerised. She lifted her free hand and stroked the baby's cheek with a finger. It was so soft.

'Oh, you are a beauty, aren't you? Yes, you are…'

Eva didn't even know what she was saying. Nonsense. She felt herself relaxing. Allowing the baby to settle more into the crook of her arm. She felt the same yearning sensation she always did when she saw children or babies, but this time she had no defences to push it back down. This place…the last few days…the intensity between her and Vidal…had left her exposed.

And now, with this beautiful baby in her arms, she couldn't fight the truth any more. She was undone. She wanted a baby. She wanted a family. She wanted to be healed by the love of a family. She wanted Vidal. She loved Vidal—even though he would never choose her or love her.

'You're a natural.'

Eva looked to her side. Vidal had come to sit beside her. It was as if he'd intuited that she was at her most raw and appeared to make her feel even more exposed.

He frowned. 'You're crying.'

'Am I?' Eva half laughed, half cried. She didn't care. The baby's tiny fist closed around her little finger and she said, almost to herself, 'I always thought I didn't want this…that maybe I couldn't have it. But I do want it.'

The baby mewled again and this time she didn't stop, working herself up into a full-blown cry.

Eva panicked. 'I don't know what to do—'

Vidal deftly took the baby out of her arms and lifted her so that she was draped over his shoulder. He patted her back and after a moment the baby burped.

He looked at Eva. 'She just had some wind.'

Seriously impressed, Eva said, 'Since when do you know about babies?'

Vidal's voice was dry. 'Since Hal has been coming to work on the house and hands me whichever child or baby he's been left to mind that day.'

Chelle appeared again and took the baby back, holding her with that expert ease that Eva could only envy. The baby smiled gummily.

Chelle said, 'It's time for the cake—come on.'

For the rest of the evening Eva couldn't ignore her revelations. She loved Vidal. She wanted a family. She knew instinctively that that was the only way she would be fully healed after the childhood she'd had.

But she'd already told Vidal too much. He was quiet. Distracted. No doubt horrified by Eva's show of emotion and her confession.

When they got back to the house he said, 'I have to make some calls. We'll be leaving in the morning.'

'Oh...okay. Back to San Francisco?'

'Madrid, actually. There's an event to attend. If that's okay with you?'

Eva balked at that. Going back to Madrid? What was even there for her any more?

What is there anywhere?

She ignored the self-pitying voice. 'Of course. That's fine.'

Eva was asleep on a reclined seat on the opposite side of the aisle in the plane. She'd refused Vidal's offer to use the bedroom. The steward had pulled a blanket over her and Vidal had had to restrain himself from snarling at him to let *him* do it. He was jealous, and he'd never been jealous over a woman in his life.

When he'd seen Eva holding Chelle's baby at the party it had stopped him in his tracks. The look on her face...

At first it had been abject terror and horror, and he'd told himself he shouldn't be surprised, because that was exactly the reaction he would have expected from Eva.

But then her expression had softened and changed. Had become one of wonder.

She'd cried.

And she'd admitted that she wanted a baby. And it hadn't been said with any kind of coquettishness. Or for his benefit. He'd have had to be blind not to see that she was literally admitting that fact to herself for the first time.

And that was the moment when he'd known that this had gone too far. Eva *was* different now. He'd been punishing her for crimes she'd committed while under the influence of a very malevolent presence.

Even Chelle had seen it. She'd pulled him aside while Eva had been talking to one of Chelle's friends and had said, 'That is a very special girl, Vidal. But she's been wounded by life. Don't hurt her any more than she already has been.'

Vidal had been stunned by the fact that one of his best friends was not only defending Eva but warning him off her! But he'd realised that he couldn't in all conscience keep up this charade of a relationship. His and Eva's past had been well and truly exorcised. He'd indulged in every fantasy he'd ever had about her. She'd changed. She wasn't the girl he'd known. Or thought he'd known.

But you still want her.

Vidal looked away from Eva's sleeping form. It was just lust. It would fade. He needed to move on and find the woman he would marry.

CHAPTER TEN

MADRID IN THE autumn was magical. The city was bathed in bright sunshine and russet and gold. Eva marvelled that she really didn't know the city well at all. Maybe, when all this was done, she'd come here and pretend she was a tourist.

She smiled at that thought.

'What's funny?'

Eva looked at Vidal on the other side of the car. 'Nothing…just thinking nonsense.'

Vidal looked serious. Eva was tempted to ask if everything was okay, but she wasn't sure if she wanted to know the answer. He had been distant since the party on Maui. He hadn't touched her, and her body literally ached from being so close to his but not touching.

They'd arrived at dawn that morning. She'd been surprised to find that Vidal had booked them into the penthouse suite of a different hotel from the one he'd stayed in the last time. When she'd asked him about it he'd said, 'I thought you might appreciate not revisiting where you used to work.'

His thoughtfulness had touched her.

They'd had breakfast and changed, and now were on their way to Eva's solicitor's office to sign final contracts and make sure all loose ends were tied up.

Eva couldn't help feeling that they'd come full circle, somehow...

After their meeting with the solicitor, Vidal waited for Eva to get back into the car, but she stopped. 'Actually, I think I'll walk back. I might go to a museum. Or an art gallery...'

Vidal frowned. 'Why?'

Eva shrugged. 'Why not?'

She held her breath for a second, wondering if he might join her, but he just said, 'As you wish. You need to be back at the hotel by four to meet the stylist and her team and get ready.'

Eva hid her disappointment. 'What is the event later?'

'It's for a charity that funds cancer research.'

Her heart constricted. No doubt he was interested in that because of his father.

She said, 'Okay, I won't be late.'

Vidal got back into the car and watched as Eva crossed the road and started walking. She was wearing dark trousers and a cashmere jumper under a light coat. Flat shoes. Hair pulled back into a low bun. Dark sunglasses.

She looked like any other stylish Madrileña, walking in the sunshine, but Vidal didn't see any others—he saw only her.

The car turned at some lights and Eva disappeared around a corner, and for a second a sense of panic almost overwhelmed Vidal. He'd wanted to go with her—to a gallery or a museum. But at the last second he'd realised that he couldn't. Because this relationship was not about that…and it was coming to an end.

They'd both benefited. It was time for him to let Eva go.

Eva got back to the hotel in good time. She'd enjoyed her walk and had visited a gallery and stopped for coffee. She hadn't been able to shake the feeling of loneliness, though, and she cursed herself. It wasn't as if she wasn't used to it. And it wasn't as if her relationship with Vidal had ever been about going on dates like normal people.

She arrived at the same time as the stylist and her team, and braced herself for the ordeal of being dressed up and done up. But the dress had the power to make her stop in her tracks.

If she'd ever dreamed of being a princess,

then this was the dress. It was a gown of sheer tulle, covered with gems, with a diamanté and gold belt around her waist. The stylist kept her hair down and smoothed it into sleek waves. Her make-up was a little more dramatic than usual, with kohl around her eyes and deep red lipstick.

Eva saw herself in the mirror and thought how proud her mother would be if she could see her now. Looking every inch the glittering heiress. Except she'd never really been an heiress to much at all. That was the sad truth. Heiress of a tainted legacy.

She noticed the stylist and the other women around her collectively doing a double take, and one of them blushed profusely. Eva turned around. Vidal was in the doorway, fixing his cufflinks. He was wearing a tuxedo, this time with a white jacket and black bow tie. It made him look even darker and more gorgeous.

Eva could sympathise with the love-struck women.

He looked up and saw her, and for the first time since they'd left Maui she felt a spurt of hope when she saw how his eyes darkened and his jaw clenched. He might not be touching her, but he wanted to.

'You look stunning, Eva. Truly.'

Now she was blushing. 'Thank you.'

The stylist and her team gathered up their

things and said goodbye. Eva thanked them profusely, appreciating so much that she didn't have
to figure out all this stuff on her own.

When they were alone, Vidal said, 'Actually,
there's something I want to talk to you about before we go. Let's have an aperitif?'

Eva followed him into the suite's reception
room. He poured her a glass of white wine and
himself a small whisky. She took the glass.
'Thank you.'

The sun was setting on Madrid, and with its
autumnal colours the city looked as if it was on
fire.

She lifted her chin. An old reflex. 'What is it
you want to talk about?'

But she already knew. It was in every line of
Vidal's body. Tense. Rejecting.

This was it.

He said, 'It's good news, actually. I've got the
investment I was looking for—for my project.
I'm going to go back to the States tomorrow, to
New York, to meet with the investors and sign
contracts. You were instrumental in that, Eva,
so thank you.'

'But I didn't do anything.'

Vidal shook his head. 'You did far more than
you realise. People were charmed by you. Especially Sophia Brentwood and her husband—
which led more or less directly to this result.'

Eva's face felt hot. 'But I didn't even know who they were.'

'Yet you charmed them.'

'I didn't know I could do such a thing. I feel like for my whole life I was being instructed *not* to charm anyone for fear of looking weak.'

'It would appear you have an innate ability to connect with people,' Vidal said, his tone dry. 'Trust it, Eva. Your mother didn't kill your spirit.'

That made her feel ridiculously emotional. 'Thank you…that's a nice thing to say.' Then she thought of what he'd said at the start. She looked at him. 'You said you're going back to New York? You don't need me to come?'

Vidal shook his head. 'No, I don't. After tonight, this arrangement is over.'

Eva felt as if he'd slapped her. Her ears were ringing. Somehow she managed to say, 'Why do you need me tonight, then?'

'Because it's a high-profile event. I can release a statement in the next few days, saying that we've parted amicably after our short engagement.'

'After you sign the contracts for the investment, presumably?'

'That would be prudent…yes.'

The sheer depth of his cold ruthlessness made her breathless. 'So you're just planning on leaving me here like some kind of…left luggage?'

'You deserve to have your life back. Free of debts or ties.'

She'd be tied to Vidal for the rest of her life and he didn't even know it. She knew there could be no other man for her.

'What if I refuse to go tonight?'

Vidal shrugged. 'That's entirely your choice. I'd prefer if you did, as it's a high-profile event, but it won't make much difference to the statement.'

'Why tell me now and not afterwards? That way you would have been assured of my co-operation.'

'Because I didn't want you to think I'd manipulated you.'

'That's noble of you.' Eva was only half mocking.

He looked at her. 'It's not as if we didn't know how this was going to go.'

Eva did her best to look unconcerned. 'Of course.' Then, 'As for the other...the fact that we became lovers...'

Vidal's face became a smooth mask. 'I see no justification in prolonging a temporary affair.'

Certainly no justification as base as prolonging it because they both wanted it. Vidal had had his fun, made his deal, taken his revenge, and he was now ready to move on. Eva could almost admire his clinical efficiency.

She wondered if this was what he was like with all his lovers. Handing them a glass of wine before going out for the evening and telling them coolly and dispassionately that it was over.

Well, Eva refused to be the kind of woman who stormed off in a huff or threw her glass of wine over him—much as she was tempted to right now. Instead, she called on every ounce of the armour she hadn't had to use in some time. She took a sip of wine and put the glass down, then said coolly, 'I'm ready. Shall we go?'

Vidal looked at her for a long moment. Eva met his look. She prayed with every fibre of her being that he was buying her act. Because inside she was breaking into a million pieces.

He drained his glass and put it down. 'Very well…let's go.'

Somehow Eva managed to get through the evening. Her first public event back among her peers in Madrid. The same people who had laughed at her all those years ago, giving her a complex.

Now, they couldn't get enough of her. Air-kissing and declaring that they must meet soon for lunch/coffee/drinks…

She couldn't think of anything worse. She felt as if the walls were closing in on her. She thought of Vidal's open glass house in San Francisco, or his beautiful mountain-top house in Maui and wished she was there, feeling free.

But she wasn't. Because they weren't her homes. She didn't belong there.

Thankfully, just when her feet were starting to scream and her face was aching from forcing smiles, they left.

The journey in the car back to the hotel was silent. Vidal had touched her during the evening, but only the most solicitous of touches. Like a stranger. He might still want her, but not enough. And did she want him to string it out just for the sake of it?

Pathetically, Eva knew that if Vidal suggested continuing the affair, she would probably say yes.

He was doing her a favour by letting her retain her dignity.

Vidal had taken off his jacket and waistcoat and tie, feeling constricted. He paced up and down in the suite. Everything he'd said to Eva earlier had been with the view of doing her a favour. Releasing her from this charade so she could get on with her life and not be beholden any more.

So why didn't it feel like a good thing? Why had it left him feeling edgy and restless and volatile?

Because of the look on her face when he'd

told her he didn't need her any more. Shock. And something else that he hadn't been able to decipher.

Of course it would look better if they stayed together for a while longer—a month at least. To let news of the deal sink in. And of course he still wanted her. So much that it had taken all his control to only touch her fleetingly all night. It had been excruciating not to be able to search for and find her hand. Slip his arm around her waist. Smell her scent. Imagine peeling that exquisite dress from her body and making her melt under his hands. Again and again.

But now that he knew everything he couldn't in all conscience keep up the charade. Eva deserved more.

She appeared in the doorway behind him and he saw her reflected in the window. She'd taken off the dress and she was wearing jeans and a top. Carrying a small suitcase.

He turned around. 'Where are you going?'

'I don't see the point in staying. I'm going back to the *castillo*. I believe it's still mine for two weeks? I need to clear out some things anyway.'

Vidal felt a sense that he was falling. 'I booked this suite for you for a month, or however long you need it—until you get your bearings.'

Eva shook her head. 'That wasn't necessary, but thank you.'

Vidal, rarely at a loss, felt at a loss now.

Eva smiled, but it was small. 'Thank you, Vidal, for freeing me from the burden of my inheritance. And for showing me the world. And for...' She stopped there.

Vidal's gut clenched. He felt ashamed. 'You don't have to thank me. I all but blackmailed you into this charade.'

She shook her head. 'I had a choice. It wasn't your fault the *castillo* wasn't selling, and I'm sure it would have eventually. It was no hardship being treated to a life of luxury and glamour. And you didn't have to blackmail me into your bed. I wanted to be there.'

Like in that moment when Vidal had felt humbled before Eva's innocence, he felt humbled again.

She said, 'I wish you well, Vidal. Truly. You deserve to find the woman you'll love and marry her and have your family.'

The thought of that now felt like grit in his mouth. 'You deserve all that too.'

Eva smiled again, but it looked sad. 'I'm sure some day I'll find my people. The ones I really want to be with. They aren't here, in this society, and you've helped me to see that.'

It was a statement Vidal would never have expected to hear this woman make. He'd misjudged her and underestimated her. She deserved her freedom now.

'Let my driver take you to the *castillo*, at least.'

'Okay, thank you.'

And then, she was gone.

Vidal heard the door closing.

He went through the suite to the bedroom, where the evening gown was neatly hanging in its protective bag. Something caught his eye and he saw the engagement ring sitting on the top of a chest of drawers. He went over and picked it up, pressed it into the palm of his hand. He curled his fingers around it so tightly that the gemstones dug into his skin painfully.

He had no right to demand anything else of Eva Flores. He had to let her go. Their past was well and truly exorcised.

About a week later, Eva was in old cut-off shorts and a sleeveless shirt tied at her waist in a knot. Hair tucked up under a baseball cap. Sneakers on her feet so old they had holes in them.

It was unseasonably warm and she wanted to swim in the pool, but the surface was covered in leaves and debris, so she was using a brush to clear it.

She leant forward as much as she could, holding the brush, and then a voice came from nearby.

'Careful.'

Eva might have fallen in if her whole body hadn't frozen on the spot. She'd been hearing Vidal's voice all week, in whispers and echoes around the *castillo*. But this sounded uncomfortably real. Maybe she really was losing it?

She straightened up and looked around. The sun was in her eyes, so all she could see was a tall, broad shape. Much like the first day he'd appeared again.

He stepped forward and she could see him now. Dressed in a three-piece suit. She was afraid to do anything or say anything in case he vapourised. Then she thought about how she looked right now, and of him in his pristine suit.

She gestured between them. 'I think if anything demonstrates how karma works, this is it.'

'No amount of casual clothes or menial tasks can hide true breeding.'

Now she knew he wasn't an apparition. She put the brush down and took off the gloves she'd been wearing to gather up dead leaves and dirt.

'Why are you here, Vidal?'

'Because it took me a week to realise that I'd made a huge mistake.'

Eva's heart palpitated. 'A huge mistake about what?'

'I should never have let you go. Or at the

very least that I should have asked you what you want.'

'What I want…?' Eva said faintly.

Vidal came closer. He had an intense expression on his face. 'What *do* you want, Eva?'

What do I want?

Where did she start? A spark of anger ignited. He was toying with her again. She put her hands on her hips. 'It wasn't enough for you to get your revenge? You've come back for more?'

'What do you want, Eva?' he repeated.

Anger mixed with other volatile emotions. What he was asking her was huge. No one had ever asked her what she wanted. Never. She'd been used as a pawn by her mother and then by this man.

Except was that really fair? He hadn't forced her into anything. He'd just presented her with an opportunity. If she hadn't fallen into his bed—jumped!—it would have been a business deal, albeit unorthodox. She would have walked away intact. In every sense.

The fact that she hadn't was down to her as much as him.

And the fact that Vidal was here, in front of her, back at the place where she'd first seen him, made something crumble inside Eva.

She had no defences left. She'd teased this man and she'd tested his patience. She'd treated him like a lesser being.

'What do I want, Vidal?' She put her hands out, 'What I want is to be forgiven by you. What I want is to be far away from this place. I can't breathe here. The only place I can breathe is with you.'

Vidal came even closer. The intense expression on his face didn't change. His eyes were burning. 'There is nothing to forgive unless you're prepared to forgive me too. The truth is that I love you, Eva. And I think I've loved you from the start, when you drove me so crazy I couldn't see straight.'

Eva felt light-headed. 'I didn't mean to…'

'But you did. And I wouldn't change it for anything.'

Vidal came closer.

'How can you say that? I was a brat.'

He shook his head. 'A beautiful, maddening brat. And underneath that brat was this even more beautiful woman, waiting to find herself and emerge.'

Eva's eyes stung. 'You don't mean it. You… you can't just appear here and say that.'

He lifted a hand and touched her face with his fingers…the barest touch, but it burned.

'Why not? You're the one, Eva. You've always been the one. You never left me. You haunted me for years. I was always going to come back because I couldn't *not*. I think my father knew that there was something between us. I think he engineered it so that I'd have to come back and find you.'

Eva's chin lifted. Old habits died hard. 'You said I was the last woman in the world you'd marry.'

'I was wrong—and cruel. The truth is that you're the *only* woman in the world I'd marry.'

She shook her head. She'd been on her own for so long. She'd never been loved. What Vidal was saying...offering...as much as she wanted it, it terrified her.

'You can't, Vidal. There's something wrong with me. That's why my parents couldn't love me. You'll see...'

Vidal reached for her baseball cap and pulled it off. Her hair fell down around her shoulders and back. He cupped her face in his hands. His familiar scent washed through her.

'No, my love. There was something wrong with *them.* They were twisted. They were bad parents.'

Fear rose up inside Eva. 'What if I am too? You deserve someone who can give you a happy family, Vidal. I don't know if—'

He kissed her, stopping her words. Then pulled back. '*I* know. You deserve to be happy too, Eva. And if we have a family we will be happy...and if we don't we will be happy. Because all I need is you.'

'I'm not imagining this?'

'No—and I'm not leaving without you. As long as you want this too.'

Eva was slowly allowing herself to believe that Vidal was real...that this was real. That the joy spreading through her was real.

'I want this to be real so badly it scares me,' she said.

'It is. Believe me. And I have something for you.'

He let her go briefly, to take something out of his pocket. Eva looked down. It was the engagement ring. He took her hand and slipped the ring back onto her finger.

'What happens now?' she asked.

Vidal smiled at her. 'We leave this place and the past behind us. How does that sound?'

Joy bubbled up inside Eva and she let out a little laugh and a hiccup. 'That sounds good. Almost too good to be true. I'm scared, Vidal... Scared that this isn't really happening. That I'm just dreaming this up. This moment... I fantasised about you taking me away from here so many times when I was younger...'

A mischievous glint came into his eye. 'I know how to reassure you that it's very real.'

Eva frowned, and then opened her mouth to ask *How?* But she never got to say it because Vidal had taken her hand and jumped fully clothed into the pool, pulling Eva with him.

She rose to the surface, spluttering and laughing and in shock at what he had just done. Vidal broke the surface too and reached for her, two big hands on her waist, tugging her into him.

She wrapped her legs around his waist and her arms around his neck. 'You're crazy!'

He grinned. 'Now do you believe it's real?'

Eva grinned too. She couldn't help it. It fizzed up and out of her. She nodded. 'Yes, I believe.'

Vidal moved them so that her back was against the side of the pool. He took his hands from Eva's waist and started undoing the buttons on her shirt. He pulled the lace cups of her bra down and exposed her breasts to his gaze. The water was cold, but Eva was boiling.

Vidal asked, 'Did I ever tell you about the fantasy I used to have about making love to you in this pool?'

She nodded. 'You might have mentioned it in passing...'

Before he could distract her with his far too wicked mouth, she cupped his face and said emotionally, 'It was always you, Vidal. No one else could have saved me.'

He kissed her. A kiss of benediction. 'You don't need saving—you need to be loved. And I am going to spend my life showing you how worthy you are of love. But I need you to love me too, because that's all I've ever wanted.'

Eva smiled. 'Is that all? That's easy...'

EPILOGUE

San Francisco

VIDAL WALKED THROUGH the house. The sun was setting and the Golden Gate Bridge in the distance stood out against the blazing sky. He would have stopped to admire the view, but it came a distant second to everything else he had to admire in his life now.

He stopped at the door of his office and admired his favourite view. Eva's head was in her hand and she was poring over a document, wearing new reading glasses that made her look even sexier, if that was possible. Especially when she had her hair up in a messy top-knot and was wearing an off-the-shoulder slouchy top and cut-off jeans. Bare legs and feet.

Who would have known that underneath her *froideur* the princess of the *castillo* was at heart a California girl? She'd even started learning to surf on Maui, and they went back there as much as possible.

This last year had been a revelation. Vidal had realised how hubristic he'd been in assuming he could attain the kind of love that his parents had shared. What they'd shared had been unique. To them. He'd limited himself in wanting what they'd had.

What he shared with Eva was so far beyond what he might have imagined or hoped for. She humbled him every day with the journey she'd taken from what had been an abusive childhood. Something he'd only fully appreciated over time. As had she. With the help of therapy she was finally coming to terms with her complicated relationship with her mother and father.

He couldn't wait any longer. He cleared his throat, wondering if he should be insulted that her studies for a degree in economics and business were more absorbing than him.

She looked up and smiled. Every time she smiled now it made Vidal emotional. So he was emotional a lot. But he took such joy in her healing.

'There you are,' she said.

Vidal smiled too. 'Here I am. Wife.'

'Husband.'

'Love of my life.'

Eva rolled her eyes but kept smiling. 'Ugh… so soppy.'

He came into the room. 'You'll pay for that, Mrs Suarez.'

She stood up and reached for him, wrapping her arms around his neck, her mouth seeking and finding the tender spot just under his ear. She breathed against him. 'Mrs Suarez… I like that a lot. So much more than Flores.'

She pulled back and Vidal took her glasses off, putting them aside. At the feel of her curves against his body he almost forgot his objective. But then he remembered. 'I have something for you upstairs.'

She stopped him for a moment. 'Actually… there's something I need to tell you.'

She looked a little apprehensive, but also excited.

Vidal asked, 'Can it wait?'

After a moment she nodded. 'Yes, it can wait.'

He took her by the hand and led her out and up to the next level. To the terrace, where there was a large box with a bow on top.

'You know you don't have to get me things,' Eva grumbled behind him. 'I have so much stuff I don't even know what to do with it all.'

'Hush, you ungrateful wench.'

There was also an ice bucket with a bottle of

champagne in it and two frosted glasses on the low table.

Eva stopped. 'What have I forgotten? Our anniversary? But that's not till next month. Your birthday? That was last month. My birthday isn't until April…'

Vidal put a hand over her mouth. 'It doesn't have to be any occasion. Be patient, my love.'

He led her over and sat her down on one of the seats near the box. Then he crouched down beside it. 'This is a gift I've been meaning to get you for some time…but I was waiting for the perfect… Well, you'll see…'

They'd started trying for a baby not long after their wedding, with Vidal reassuring Eva that she would be an amazing mother. But so far each month had passed with no pregnancy. Vidal knew that Eva was a little worried, even though she wasn't saying anything. So he wanted to give her something to distract her.

'What is it, Vidal?'

He took the top off the box and lifted out a small, furry, wriggling bundle of…

'A puppy!' Eva squealed, reaching for it immediately.

The fluffy golden retriever puppy, delighted to be liberated from the box, promptly weed on Eva and licked her face with enthusiastic kisses.

Eva laughed, and then started crying, clinging on to the creature.

Vidal sat beside her, concerned. 'I didn't want to make you cry.'

She shook her head and buried her face in the puppy. Then looked up again, her face wreathed in smiles. 'Happy tears. I've always wanted a dog.'

Vidal wiped away her tears with his thumbs. 'I know, and I've wanted to get you one for so long. I know we've been trying for a baby, and I know you're worried even though you haven't said anything, but I don't want you to be because I'm sure—'

Eva put a hand over Vidal's mouth. The puppy was squirming to be free and Vidal took him from Eva. She took her hand down.

He said, 'What?'

She glanced at the champagne on ice and back to Vidal, and then smiled tremulously, more tears forming. 'I don't think I'll be able to have any of that for a while.'

It took a few seconds for Eva's meaning to sink in. And then he remembered her saying she needed to tell him something. In a daze, he said, 'This is what you wanted to tell me?'

She nodded and took his hand. The puppy slithered off Vidal's lap and started sniffing around the terrace. They were oblivious.

Vidal couldn't say anything—and then he couldn't stop. 'Are you sure? When? How long? How?'

Eva laughed and placed his hand on her still-flat belly. 'I'm about six weeks. I missed a period and didn't want to say anything just in case. But I went to the doctor today. It's early days... She's sure everything is fine, but obviously we have to be careful.'

Vidal took his hand from Eva's belly and cupped her face. He was so full of joy he wasn't sure how he wasn't exploding with it. He said, 'You are going to be an amazing mother, Eva, and you are going to give our child all the love that you didn't have.'

She smiled, and it was watery. He saw in it a mix of joy and trepidation. 'I don't know about that...but I do know that with you as its father we can't go wrong.'

Vidal shook his head. 'Have faith, my love... you'll see.'

And approximately thirty-four weeks later Eva *did* see. She held their dark-haired daughter, Inez, in her arms and she'd never felt such an infusion of pure love and devotion. She knew she would die for this child. She would never harm her.

Maybe her mother had felt like this when Eva had been born, but somewhere along the way she'd become twisted. Eva knew deep in her bones that she was different. She was stronger. And that was perhaps the biggest gift of all.

One day, not long after Inez had been born, they were walking along the beach at sunset. The baby was nestled against Vidal's chest in a sling. Eva was bone-tired but had never been more content. Their beloved mischievous dog, Toto, sped after a ball in the surf—his favourite pastime apart from guarding baby Inez.

They were just one in a number of similar families on the beach at this hour. It was a simple moment, but so profound. And it impacted on Eva so deeply that she had to stop and let it wash through her.

Vidal looked at her and smiled. He picked up her hand and pressed a kiss to her palm.

'Thank you,' she said, and there was a wealth of meaning and love in those two innocuous words.

He shook his head. 'Thank *you*. I thought I knew what love was, but I had no idea.'

'And I didn't know what it was at all!' Eva half laughed and half cried.

But now she did. And so did Vidal. And that was all they needed to know.

Eva wrapped her arms around Vidal's waist and they continued their walk, melting into the sunset and into a lifetime of true love.

* * * * *

Enchanted by A Ring for the
Spaniard's Revenge?

*Don't miss these other stories
by Abby Green!*

Bride Behind the Desert Veil
The Flaw in His Red-Hot Revenge
Bound by Her Shocking Secret
Their One-Night Rio Reunion
The Kiss She Claimed from the Greek

Available now!